PRAISE F
Riots I Have

* * * *

**Named one of the Best Books of the Year
by Electric Literature and The Marshall Project**

"Chapman's book is one of the funniest American novels to come around in years, a sharp satire of the literary scene as well as the broken prison system. Despite the grim subject matter, Chapman packs more laughs into 128 pages than most sitcoms do in an entire season."

—NPR

"If you're part of the Venn diagram that subscribes to *n+1* and *McSweeney's*, this is the funniest book you'll read all year."

—*The Washington Post*

"Darkly hilarious."

—*Newsday*

"Fitfully funny and murderously wry. . . . A frenzied yet wistful monologue from a lover of literature under siege."

—*Kirkus Reviews*

"A smart, biting take on the penal system, and a fiery ode to the power of the written word."

—*Town & Country*

"Chapman's smart, freewheeling first novel sends up both prison and literary life."

—*Seattle Metropolitan Magazine*

"Chapman's bravura performance is piquant, rollicking, and richly provoking."

—*Booklist*

"Savage, fearless, and funny as hell, *Riots I Have Known* also possesses, not so strangely, a poignant core. In this mother of all editor's notes, Ryan Chapman creates a narrative voice that is by turns tender, cruel, profane, wildly inventive and, finally, unforgettable."

—Sam Lipsyte, *New York Times* bestselling author of *Hark* and *The Ask*

RIOTS I HAVE KNOWN

RYAN CHAPMAN

Simon & Schuster Paperbacks
New York   London   Toronto   Sydney   New Delhi

Simon & Schuster Paperbacks
An Imprint of Simon & Schuster
1230 Avenue of the Americas
New York, NY 10020

First Simon & Schuster paperback edition November 2020

SIMON & SCHUSTER PAPERBACKS and colophon are registered trademarks of Simon & Schuster, Inc.

For information about special discounts for bulk purchases, please contact Simon & Schuster Special Sales at 1-866-506-1949 or business@simonandschuster.com.

The Simon & Schuster Speakers Bureau can bring authors to your live event. For more information or to book an event, contact the Simon & Schuster Speakers Bureau at 1-866-248-3049 or visit our website at www.simonspeakers.com.

Interior design by Carly Loman

Manufactured in the United States of America

10 9 8 7 6 5 4 3 2 1

Library of Congress Cataloging-in-Publication Data is available.

ISBN 978-1-5011-9730-7
ISBN 978-1-5011-9731-4 (pbk)
ISBN 978-1-5011-9733-8 (ebook)

"How am I not myself?"

—Jude Law, *I Heart Huckabees*

Lopez, right before they stabbed him in the yard—this was maybe last winter or the winter previous—you know what he said? He said: "Time makes fools of us all." To say it at the end—he knew it was the end, as he must have known and as we all must know—such clarity! Lopez cut through years of hoary usage and conferred a real sense of gravitas upon the moment. We all felt it, all of us rubbernecking in the yard. I confess I missed the casual-Friday jab to a bit of shadow from a racing cloud, it was dark and then light and Lopez was resting against the squeaky weight bench. Everyone avoided that bench, its high-pitched chirps neutered the masculinity an otherwise strong set was meant to advertise. Lopez: the bravery! Those moments stick with you, dear reader. Months later I remember watching a Brando-esque scene chewer in some Lifetime movie—it's one of the few channels we're allowed—and the actor whispered to his teary ex-wife, "Time makes fools of us all." I shook my head and exclaimed to no one in particular with surprising volume, "You don't know what you're talking about." Lopez, who was almost definitely stabbed in the yard last winter and not the winter previous, you remember from Volume I, Issue Two, "So My Chains May Weep

Tonight," that execrable short story. For readers stuck outside the pay wall, I'll summarize briefly: "Rodrigo," on a dime for arson, covers the "Southton" yard's cement square with soulful chalk portraits of a daughter he's never met. He guesses at the features: her mother's nose, his own plump cheeks, big doe eyes. Lopez wrote long, dolorous paragraphs about those drawings, drawings never trampled by fellow inmates. (Credulity: strained.) Anyway, the portrait's subject grows from infancy to young adulthood, or so Rodrigo believes; upon his release the buoyant Rodrigo receives a conveniently timed missive from his ex-wife: she aborted the fetus a week into his incarceration. (NB: The Warden loved this O. Henry–esque twist and demanded the story's inclusion. Your humble editor's protests fell on deaf ears.)

Thinking about it now, as the riot gathers momentum in A Block, and the WXHY Action News ActionCopter buzzes past in a tireless orbit, its camera surfacing whatever rabble it can find, I commend Lopez for wresting meaning out of such a trampled phrase, "Time makes fools of us all," instilling a measure of sublimity in the death act, a sublimity otherwise absent from his treacly prose. Might he be Westbrook's own Harry Crosby? Readers quick with Wikipedia will learn that Crosby, a Boston scion-cum-*flâneur*, failed as a poet but succeeded as a patron of the arts, publishing Joyce, Eliot, some other guys, he exited spectacularly with his mistress in a ritualized murder-suicide. True, Lopez was much less foppish and much more bellicose. Still, I would suggest the old impresario lives on in our departed colleague. We envy those who go out in their own way, we all hope for the same for ourselves and hubristically we all secretly expect to go out in our own way ourselves. I've seen many men, at least four, bawl and curse their attackers, be they physical, chthonic, or oncological. We expect such a response: it is common and it is natural. How am I to go? I wonder. Enviable old Lopez, he took possession of his ending there in the yard, stabbed last winter, possibly the winter before, whichever one was the year of the new jackets. He collapsed by the gates, I remember, under the small pointillist cluster of black ash on the wall where everyone stubbed their cigarettes. The tenor of my own shuffling off this mortal coil will be determined by whoever first breaks down my meager barricade here in the Will and Edith Rosenberg Media Center for Journalistic Excellence in the Penal Arts: two upended footlockers, a standard teacher's desk, a nearly complete set of *Encyclopedia Britannica*s (2006 edition), and a scrum of Aeron chairs fish-hooked over each other just so. If I am lucky it'll be Warden Gertjens first over the transom, he no doubt sympathizes with my present situation and, I would hope, admits complicity in my present situation. He could be counted on for assistance in a boost hurdling the A/C panel, knocking out the tempered double-paned glass, and running into the embrace of my fans, followers, and future lovers. Everyone else would surely stab me in the face.

I deserve it, and this is the truth, or *a* truth, and the one I claim and will verify for the scurrilous Fox News fact-checkers whose emails presently flood my in-box. I am the architect of the Caligulan melee enveloping Westbrook's galleries and flats. Must this final issue of *The Holding Pen* be my own final chapter? Can any man control the narrative of his life, even one as influential as mine? I suppose not. And so the *The Holding Pen* winds down in real time, complemented by Breaking News updates from breathless, iron-coiffed correspondents on the scene; eighty thousand tweets and counting; protests by the Appeals on the north lawn; and blush-inducing slashfic on TheWildWestbrook.com of improbable but emboldening reunions with my sweet McNairy.

Were I petty, or spiteful, or the kind to assign blame, I'd say this is all the Latin Kings' fault, an accusation supported by Diosito's narco-sonnet "Mi Corazón en Fuego y Mi Plan de Fuga" from Volume I, Issue Eight ("Journeys"). The same issue, I remember, with the popular fold-out guide to rat-tailing one's bedsheet for sliding tobacco down the flats. Spanish-speaking readers must have gleaned the Latin Kings' intentions from stanza one, to which your editor can only express irritation for having never received even a friendly word of warning. Yet I accept in full the public drubbing that is my due, however accidental and unforeseen its cause may have been, a public drubbing that will likely take the form of the aforementioned face stabbing. I wish only to spend my remaining time clearing up a few inaccuracies.

According to the threads, the riot started thirty minutes ago in the yard and somewhere inside A Block, then spread quickly from there. Aerial footage shows four Muslim Brothers, ID'd by their bloodied keffiyehs, shot down in the grass a few feet from a hole in the north-northwest fence line. As usual, the Brothers being headstrong and stupid in equal measure. #Westbrook Instagrams from curious townies reveal plumes of gray smoke from what looks like a handful of fires in A Block, doubtless the flamers are having the most outright fun today. Of course, the fires are nothing a wall-mounted extinguisher couldn't handle, but there's never one when you need it, and anyway, those things are like gold in the present crisis-driven economy. The helicopter cameras are also picking up a group of skinheads—Steve? Looks like Steve—chucking screws' bodies out of the cafeteria skylight into a haphazard levee on the outside wall. How did they reach the skylight? I wonder. For all their rehashed lectures on miscegenation, those guys sure are inventive.

HuffPost has a top-of-the-fold photo of the north corridor windows, hidden behind a stretched bedsheet bearing a message written in what looks like oven grease: "Under the Paving Stones, Parole!" By the angle of their cameras I can surmise the news crews have camped out on the dead stretch of land to the northwest, in front of the yard. Surely the GSSR, with their ambulance-chaser's gift for opportunism, is somewhere close. I hesitate to mention them (and their unknown/"unknowable" acronym). Let's move on.

If you're watching the footage from WXHY, you have a sense of Westbrook's blueprint. Readers have remarked upon the cognitive dissonance between the Westbrook of the mind and the Westbrook of the eye. The prison is not unlike a child's snow angel, with his left arm forming A Block, his head B Block, and his right arm C Block, laid out facing east; Central Booking, Times Square, and the Infirmary in the chest; offices, the cafeteria, and the library in the crotch; and D Block and E Block as the lower appendages. For the completist, I suppose A visitor's center would be the left armpit and D visitor's center the spleen, and the Will and Edith Rosenberg Media Center for Journalistic Excellence in the Penal Arts the big toe of the right foot. (A rather propitious big toe, I should say, as this remote corner may just grant me the time I need.)

Some of you are right to ask about the much-ballyhooed F Block, which, to torture the analogy further, lay a hundred yards west like a discarded boot, composed of I-beams and pallets of cement blocks covered by weather-beaten tarps. Warden Gertjens, ever the optimist, had hoped to assemble a deluxe "front of house" for the good-behaviors and, fingers crossed, a tax-deductible location for Wes Anderson's *Folsom Fantasia*. The latest news from

Albany is no news: only the Diller Scofidio + Renfro toolshed has been completed, paid for with donations by the wife of some pharma CMO, and, in a bit of a stalemate, the governor's waiting on Michael Kimmelman's review of said toolshed before releasing capital funds. I've seen F Block's blueprints and can attest to its scope and ambition, in particular the motif of elongated curved hallways, which, Warden Gertjens said—and here I presume he's quoting the brief—"isolate one in space, removed from where one has come from and where one is going; no past, no future, only present." I feel a lachrymal swell and a priapic swell at such a vision, and tip my hat to the architects for their spatiotemporal empathy for the incarcerated. (Should the institution survive today's PR Hindenburg, naming rights are still available!)

Westbrook is the elder sibling to the new maximum-security facilities in the tri-county area, part of the construction boom for those politicians without recourse to gambling revenue. I'm told there's a recipe for installing a correctional facility on the outskirts of town; the base ingredients include one hundred unemployed blue-collar workers and a mayor with steep alimony. I confess it was a relief to be processed here just over twenty-four months ago. The main campus is careworn with the peregrinations of decades of inmates, every vertical surface marked by thousands of fingernail scratches into a deep-time calligraphic frenzy. Transfers tell us fights occur with more frequency at the new institutions, as if there were a subconscious need to fill the virginal space with local history and gobbets of injury. If I may be so bold, the difference between these prisons and Westbrook is the difference between a house and a home.

I can't smell the fires, that's a good sign. The herd hasn't spread to C Block, though I should allow for the possibility of some man-made ventilation for respiration and visibility. I'm confident I have enough time to complete my atonement and set down my reading of events as they occurred.

These riots keep to a pattern. So says Wilfred, my confidant and fount of hard-won wisdom. He survived Elmira in 1981 and Pleasant Valley in 1995 *and* 1999 completely unscathed, the old coot knows a thing or two.

He maintains three rules for these situations:

1. **Stay in your cell and lock yourself in.** Counterintuitive, yes, and against all temptation. In the rare instance someone gets to the screw station and opens the locks, it's best to tie a rolled-up sheet from the door to the window bar, doubling up if possible to ensure a taut line. Ah, you reply, but the mattress is right there! Block the gate with your mattress and they'll just smoke you out. Wilfred says dying of smoke inhalation in a prison riot is like masturbating at an orgy.

   If the riot is between you and your cell, avoid the flats, stairways, bathrooms, galleys, cafeteria, wood shop, metal shop, and all windows. Four-on-one assaults pop up like dandelions; inmates have such elephant memories.

2. **Hide your cigarettes under the bed slab.**

3. **If you possess the fortitude to knock yourself unconscious, it's a useful alibi for the exhausting post-riot investigations.** Wilfred said this was easier in his youth, when a sprint into the wall was enough to do the job. Older inmates should coordinate with a "riot buddy" to strangle each other as simultaneously as they can manage.

Were I not compelled to finish this *Holding Pen* issue/ apologia for you, I would curl up under this desk and choke myself into blissful respite. I am fortunate to have made it to the Media Center; I was midshave when I heard the call: it passed from Times Square like a caffeinated form of the telephone game, inmate by inmate, reaching me as "Jefe's pulled a coupe of tats! We're the rite of spring!" I didn't request or wait for clarification, sometimes you just have to towel off, button up your jumpsuit— I perform my morning toilet half-shod, for the increased range of motion—and dash through E Block. I fear my detractors will have one final joke at my expense, as my three-quarter neck beard will surely give my corpse an air of *non compos mentis*, despite the abundant literary evidence to the contrary. And yet, perhaps my killers will so ruinously strike me about the head, neck, and face, and then the joke will be on them.

Thinking about it now, I wonder if I've ever passed along Wilfred's advice to McNairy. I certainly wouldn't expect Wilfred to volunteer it to anyone else; I had to trade a carton of cigarettes for that three-tined fork of wisdom. (He swore there were nine more rules, but I was low.) Does McNairy know what to do? Is he safe? McNairy, my friend and companion—he's the only one who ever understood me, which is to say he understood me obliquely, he never asked questions about *The Holding Pen*, or life in Sri Lanka, or those nine blue hairs, or anything about the outside, just "Come over after work detail?" and "Do you like that?" and a question about choking, but under different circumstances. McNairy, he's the real storyteller manqué of Westbrook. Faithful readers know he never formally submitted a piece, his greater contribution was what the Teutons call his *geist*; it haunts every issue. Or perhaps a benign form of haunting, if such a word exists

in English. Yes, McNairy's naptime monologues befit the Algon-
quin Roundtable, and were I a better listener I would faithfully
transcribe here his numerous bon mots. To cite but one example:
the Protestant ethic and personal élan he brought to the hard-
line dogfighting scene of Jersey City. McNairy carved his own
niche—that is to say, Saint Bernards, plodding beasts who circled
in a hypnotic rhythm conveying, McNairy explained, I remember,
the quintessence of the sport. The dogs moved as if in slow motion, resigned and exhausted like some young ER doctor on the
tail end of a marathon shift, each bite and swipe of the paw drawing cheers from the potbellied Italians and the salt-haired blacks
of the old neighborhoods. McNairy would have been close to the
cafeteria when the riot broke out. Perhaps he's holed up in a solitary cell or fighting his way through a scrum of B Blockers—those
guys are all limbs and teeth, not a pound of muscle between the
lot of them. McNairy, be safe!

Back to the matter at hand: I feel your concerns. I feel your
concerns and I read your concerns and I promise to reply to your
concerns. The blog comments and #westbrookriot tweets are
both sobering and salutary, they cement my resolve and double
my resolve to "stay the course," as it were. I'll take this cemented
doubling and provide *the definitive account* of the rise and, it
pains me to write, the fall of *The Holding Pen*. (@blondita96 and
@marco_tized, I love you too!) While I'm naming names, I'd like
to thank Oberlin sophomore Alexis Somers for developing the
content-management system's auto-publish setting, an incredibly
useful function on days like today with their high probability of
interruption and dismemberment.

It is important to write *the definitive account*, or rather *an
official accounting of events, as they happened*. Let it be said: this

text is authoritative, sanctioned, sealed with a kiss. The reader is likely aware of the forthcoming bit of opportunism *par excellence* by Betsy Pankhurst, *Handcuffed: Sex and Madness with the Widow Killer* (Knopf), which I must stress is *the unauthorized account*, or should I say *an unauthorized account*. Resist its easy prurience! I have slogged through an advance reader's copy with rising bile, and I can objectively say it is pure slander of the lowest order. The highest order? Either way, *Handcuffed* is a fresh wound; that Betsy is my former paramour is the salt shaken liberally upon it. A cursory Google search reveals she's sold her "life rights" to Netflix in a "major deal." (More salt!) If you feel any loyalty to *The Holding Pen* and to my accomplishments—indeed, to *our* accomplishments—then you will boycott Betsy's noncanonical screed. Even here, in my last moments, the jelly of her deceit sticks to the roof of my mouth. I dwell upon the subject of Ms. Pankhurst for the sole purpose of dispelling it, and her, from our minds. Forever.

As I was saying, I believe, these riots keep to a pattern. There are rivers of mob violence, rapids of screw beatings, tributaries of looting—prescription drugs in medical, cigarettes wherever. Everyone will funnel through Central Booking in a subconscious return to whence they came—Freudians, take note—where, if Wilfred is correct, the confetti of shredded inmate files will lend things a festive air. Then a dam burst of excitement into C Block and the commissary, with men loosed from the Hole blinking a few times and, depending on their comportment, searching out friends for tear-filled reunions or pummeling whoever's close at hand. There isn't an exact science to these things, Wilfred explained, I remember, but I estimate two, maybe three hours before the crowd winds south to E Block. The Will and Edith

Rosenberg Media Center for Journalistic Excellence in the Penal Arts is at best a distraction.

But what a distraction! If I may direct the reader's attention to the Editor's Letter of Volume I, Issue Ten ("Paradise"): $4.8 million in construction, a complete gut reno of the derelict Movement Therapy studio (that shithead Fritz was the sole practitioner); locally sourced and very locally refinished tables designed by the Auerbach Brothers of Hudson, New York; the newest line of Macs with best-in-class desktop publishing software (plus Photoshop!); and all those Aeron chairs. I'm told there's a projector and screen setup that descend from a discreet envelope in the ceiling, though I haven't been able to find the remote. All of this is to say your average rioter will find only brief catharsis in vandalizing the place and, given the difficulty of battering someone with a twenty-seven-inch iMac, not much else.

I hope you will not think less of me for the unsavory measures I've had to take to protect and barricade myself in the Media Center—measures I may take again with, I fear, increasing unsavoriness. I assure you with hand over heart and other hand over keyboard I only wish to give myself more time in the service of *an official accounting of events, as they happened.* To wit: I've urinated onto the doorframe. The plastic lip bordering the carpet forms an escarpment with the hallway tile, a handy sluice for my noisome volley of psychological warfare. Or is that biological warfare? It strikes me now, as I think about it, the tactic will deter only like-minded individuals, i.e., mentally balanced individuals, and will prove futile against all others. Which begs the question: What is the efficacy of psychological warfare against the psychopath? Must I, as the Hilton Hotels advance man once advised, think as the enemy thinks? Doing so might well guarantee my safety: it would not take much imagination or labor to render this place forbiddingly disgusting were I to continue down the path of uric and fecal redoubt. But at what cost? This cost: completing my final work of literature with the clarity it demands. I will "stay the course," psychologically speaking, with the burdensome knowledge my near-term trespassers will not think twice about a piss-laden entryway. If they take notice at all, I now realize, it will provoke further enragement, serving the opposite purpose of my original intention. (One might argue the urine is an apt metaphor for this entire *Holding Pen* debacle.) But they can't kill me twice! And yet, now that I recall those involuntary courtship rituals in the showers, there's a remote but real chance the scent of urine may act as a proverbial bell to the Pavlov's dog of . . . well, I hate to put such vulgarity in print, as it were; in short, a most unwelcome "way to go." And what if I were rescued? My good fortune would be instantly compromised, and I would become the crazed fetishist micturating on high-end furniture.

To add further impugnment, on-the-scene interviews by WXHY Action News with Taghkanic police and CERT officers place the blame squarely on yours truly. Me! Your humble editor, while Diosito and the others escape scrutiny and recapture.

Not to mention Warden Gertjens. While the mantra of the embattled egotist is the immortal "The whole thing was his idea," I would be remiss if I didn't say the whole thing was his idea. In that fateful meeting last July, I sat uncomfortably in a wing-back leather chair in the Warden's office while he ranted about the arbitrariness of Albany's profligacy: $40M for a Staten Island landfill to blow its toxic air south, $9M for a new high school football stadium in the Bronx—whose fertilizer, the local adolescents quickly learned, produced a powerful hallucinogen when dried and smoked—and Warden Gertjens's favorite offender, the One Smartwatch per Child initiative for at-risk preschoolers. I confess I only half listened to all this, transfixed as I was by the view outside his windows. Between wooden blinds stained the color of dark-roast coffee, I could just make out the erotic blur of the interstate and the comet trails of long-haul semis.

You may be interested to know this was the first time I'd ever heard the Warden's voice. I'd heard stories from guys on the intake bus, caught a glimpse of the man during his cameo in the orientation video. Legend has it Warden Gertjens found his calling as a university student in The Hague after a fateful reading of Le Corbusier's journals, specifically some eight-word parenthetical aside on prisons. It was within those parentheses the young man would live—and indeed, would thrive. In the past decade he's scurried up the corrections ladder from mealy-mouthed DOC clerk to a star CPA in selvedge denim jeans (retired at the first hint of whiskering) with a stated willingness to relocate his wife and two young daughters at a moment's notice should a better position arise. He filled his intellectual diet with nightly binges of dense academic journals: *Criminal Psychology*, *Incarcerated Psychopathology*, and the brutal elegance of *Institutions*. Looking around his office, I noted framed commendations from prisons in Oklahoma, Alaska, even California. Which is not to ignore his greatest skill, the very reason for my fateful meeting. For Oot Gertjens was a born rainmaker, adept at navigating Albany's labyrinthine back channels, playing tennis with the DC machers, and defending enhanced interrogations in op-eds for *The New Republic* and *Apartamento*. The Warden was not without his flaws, of course, but unlike most visionaries he operated in an environment in which his most vocal critics could be shackled and sedated.

I snapped to attention as his speech rose in pitch. There was an unmistakable ebullience under his words, a childlike giddiness behind the probity: apparently a fence jumper in Nyack had buggered a bunch of latchkey kids. This, the Warden explained, I remember, was good news for Westbrook, as the escapee—John Ray Jones or Joe Ray Johns, something like that; you can look it up—had become an unkillable talking point for conservatives. Imus did three shows. Rush did five. (They both blamed the "soft-on-guns" guard-tower CO.) Sean Hannity organized his Million Concealed Weapons March on the National Mall. The constituency, the Warden said, pushing up the sleeves on his black turtleneck, was riled up. His tone reminded me of something I'd learned from Father Christopher—learned and then promptly forgot, and then recalled out of the blue that day in the Warden's office. That is, the tradition of the hierophant. I felt it in my chest and in my bladder: here was an interpreter of the holy.

The Warden said Senator Moser, in all her Thatcherite wisdom, was in the process of adding generous earmarks for getting tougher on crime. Though I've always considered myself something of a political agnostic, I remember nodding, I remember replying that getting tough on crime was a good idea, a great idea, the greatest idea I'd ever heard. Warden Gertjens then outlined a new prison newsletter: a journal of the arts "sympathetic to the incarcerated subject and the reforms unique to Westbrook."

I was now the editor in chief of a one-man editorial department. This was motivation enough to do my very best, and naturally I was well suited to it: my Jesuit education was a pronounced advantage in a job market of subliterates and philistines. The Warden also cited my lack of gang affiliation and—here he consulted some papers on his desk—my psych eval's Rubin test indicated I was a Questioner, a rarity among the local population. If I grant myself a moment of self-flattery, it should be said I always "go the distance" in completing whatever task I'm charged with carrying out, I'm practically famous for it. The Warden concluded our meeting by saying failure on my part would earn ten weeks in solitary.

I should clarify: it's true that a handful of inmates dedicate themselves to betterment through distance learning and our "Reform the Future!" workshops. But these studious souls are always child rapists, and their autodidacticism is both a function of and a solution to the endless alone time suffered by the incarcerated pariah. A total waste. The smartest men at Westbrook were the same men you never wanted to talk to and wouldn't be caught dead with. From the very first issue of *The Holding Pen*, it was a matter of personal integrity to never publish their submissions— even though, as you would expect, their work showed the highest literary merit. At this moment these blighted scholars are likely somewhere in C Block experiencing a robust bludgeoning, the pedos are just magnets for abuse. I admit to a slight wince when I think of their work, forever lost to the dustbin of history.

(In response to @JenGrrrl98's tweet: Do we enjoy *Annie Hall* less, knowing its director, writer, and star conducted sexual relations with his adopted daughter? And if we do enjoy it less, what of the contrast between the filmmaker's moral ugliness and the very existence of his lauded artistic creation? Might this tension create an aesthetic criterion unique to the work and its ilk? Might we then enjoy less those otherwise "normal" entertainments by artists we've deemed faultless, cognizant—as we must be—of the absence of this new tension? And what might faultless mean in such context? It is an almost comic judgment, relying purely on the biographical information available to us, which, if impeccable, cannot be anything but partial. [In response to @JenGrrrl98's response: charges of "the pot calling the kettle black" only further proves my thesis.])

As for my own artistic position, it is undoubtedly shaped by the whiff of destiny that seems to accompany my adventures, misadventures, and multiple felonies. I would suggest a genetic predisposition to a life in letters, and perhaps the Warden intuited this on a subconscious or pheromonal level when he charged me with spearheading *The Holding Pen*. I would cite my paternal grandfather Eloy, by no means a learned man, who supplemented the revenue from his roadside mango stand with scuba excursions for expat Brits—at that time a degenerate lot, too louche for London but not louche enough for Tangiers. They would decamp to Ceylon, as they insisted on calling it—a name I've found degrading on a phonetic level in addition to the obvious colonial affront, sounding as it does like that anti-Semitic French novelist. Grandfather Eloy found steady work under none other than Arthur C. Clarke, a true undersea enthusiast and a true overland asshole. "Always talking," Grandfather Eloy complained.

It's possible the man's memories were colored by bitterness. He was diving with Clarke when they chanced upon the ruins of the famous Koneswaram temple, a discovery of no small archaeological importance. This was of course the same temple the Portuguese had pushed off a cliff in the 1600s, and, like Tenzing Norgay three years earlier, my grandfather received no credit in the international press. (He won local renown; in Trincomalee this is akin to being named the tallest midget.) Clarke oversaw the Hindu temple's rescue and preservation, enlisting my grandfather as a go-between for, it must be said, lucrative rates. I would argue this proximity to literature, if you will, seeped into Grandfather Eloy's DNA in some osmotic fashion, recombining over the decades and biding its time until finding expression in these very words.

Some of you might be interested in a bit of family lore. Grandfather Eloy was a stoic character. One evening, as the skiff made its way into shore, Clarke asked him what occupied his thoughts all day. "Apes fighting," Grandfather said, perhaps in jest, perhaps not. Clarke spit into his scuba mask, wiped, looked off at the receding waves, and replied: "Apes? . . . Indeed."

It appears as though the Appeals have begun a chorus of jump-rope chants to liven the mood and promote light cardiovascular exercise: news cameramen on their union breaks are joining in with impressive fleet-footedness. I can't make out the words in the Snapchat footage, but there's a positive vibe to it all. My brothers in arms, I am with you in solidarity and 4/4 time.

To counter some of the pushback re: egotism and re: post-penal-lit hegemony, *The Holding Pen* does not imply any kind of monopoly on the cultural output of Westbrook. Far from it. In fact, *The Holding Pen* wasn't the Warden's first attempt at pecuniary support via "lefty 'human interest'" stories, as he put it, I remember. For instance, there was the "I Made This!" initiative, named for a stamp on the belts exported to East Coast menswear boutiques, with accompanying tags featuring photographs of each felon "maker" in three-quarters profile, a total failure with the exception of those fashioned by Giuseppe Milani, fifth-generation leatherworker and first-generation arsonist. I believe a local garment-workers' union scuttled the project a few months into my sentence.

As for the brief run of the sandwich shop Open Faces of Death, the less said the better.

If we were to narrow our scope to literary matters, *The Holding Pen* is but the most recent in a long line of rehabilitative *écrits* here at Westbrook. There are the writings of Mookie "Jeff" Sanders, who from his incarceration in 1988 to his death in 2002 (heart attack, the lucky bastard) churned out voluminous period romances for Avon under the nom de plume Raleigh de la Cruz: *An Affair of the Heart, Scarlet Sands, The Francophone Lieutenant's Woman.* Sanders attributed his consistent sales at Bible Belt grocery stores to an unwavering formula of biracial female protagonists kidnapped by marauding pirates and, after a few chapters of lusty tension, rescue from implied sex slavery by a velvet-gloved naval officer with a nondebilitating physical weakness. (From his Rita Award acceptance speech: "Eye patches work. IBS, not so much.") And folk-art aficionados may know Cromwell Eberhardy's finger painting from the *Artforum* debate in the late 1980s: Should his work be read as abstract expressionism or, given the artist's impaired mental and visual acuity, social realism? (Criminologists know him from the 1959 Eberhardy Family Reunion shooting spree in San Luis Obispo.)

Obviously, neither of these precedents benefited from the Warden's tutelage and resources. From Matt Biddle's nine-thousand-word *Washington Post Weekend* profile, which I admit I've only skimmed: "Gertjens's Manichaean nature manifests itself publicly as a beneficent modern Rockefeller dressed down like a bobo architect, with whispers of political aspirations trailing every successful initiative. Meanwhile his callowness expresses itself via eBay bids on Wegner 'wishbone' chairs one might characterize as both promiscuous and paroxysmal, in addition to fiscally irresponsible institutional expenditures that make the Sultan of Brunei look like Suze Orman." I would never condone such defamation—Warden Gertjens has always ruled fairly, as they say—nor would I bite the hand that feeds. But if I may nibble it for a moment, it must be said the Warden was and is quite power hungry. You know the first thing he told me after he told me about *The Holding Pen*, on that epoch-defining day last July? I'm paraphrasing of course, but it was something like: "Those min-sec hippies at Bright Horizons just got themselves a *Good Morning America* segment for their Cupcakes Not Bombs program, if you can believe it." An Ivan Boesky-ish born-again, transported at great expense from New Paltz's gleaming big house on the hill to the show's Manhattan studios, sat across from George Stephanopoulos and said, in the clear cadences of the media-trained, "I want to repay my debt to society in trade: if Iran will halt its nuclear production facilities, my fellow inmates and I will send every man, woman, and child in Tehran a delicious, gluten-free cupcake." Those words actually came out of the prisoner's mouth, on national television no less, Warden Gertjens said, I remember. (You can visit the *GMA* site and watch it yourself.) Cupcakes Not Bombs even received a generous NEA grant; a bit of fundraising jujitsu the Warden admitted he found novel and worthy a modicum of respect. As for Westbrook: he wanted to think bigger, something with exponential PR opportunities. How was Warden Gertjens to know *The Holding Pen* would become his undoing? He was quite narrow-minded— narrow-minded and self-interested to a (sizable) fault.

The Holding Pen is greater than Westbrook, your humble editor included, and as Sherman's March rages through B Block and C Block—or more specifically Sherman's Parade of Stabbing and Looting—it is important to consider the *The Holding Pen* in toto as a work of literature, with the appropriate critical framework this phrase implies and connotes and perhaps even denotes. A critical framework that is better imagined as, say, a critical lattice-work or, if you will, a critical *escalier* of faddish hermeneutics, correctional epistemologies, and Pinter-esque moments of silence during Slate podcasts: "Today's topic, gentlemen: Who is the incarcerated man in the twenty-first century?" "Well, Dana, isn't he . . . all of us?" Each of these threads, or, I suppose, all of these threads reticulate in a critical trellis up to the lofty balcony of understanding. We all know it is not true understanding we find on that balcony but a mere peek—and, sprouting up from the balcony floor, another critical latticework, vertiginous and hackles-raising, unnerving, seductive . . . the seduction, I would aver, of a work of literature.

One need look no further than the poetry that inspired the riot in the first place. If that's the right word, "inspired." It is a well-established fact 99.99 percent of penal verse is awful, the inbred cousin of slam poetry with the emotional range of a Wikipedia stub. Which shows you just how much the Latin Kings' piece surprised me in the most pleasant way, and by that I mean the writing itself, not their submission process, which was decidedly unpleasant and need not be discussed.

There was an aspirational current to the language, a sense of (dare I say?) spiritual possibility untethered from their shopworn Roman Catholicism, and yet grounded by a rawness at the verse's core: nobody would confuse it for poetry composed on the outside. Crucial to all of this was the acknowledgment of moral consequence, elevating the work above self-pity or self-congratulation. (Please, God, no more "street cred" villanelles!) Copy editing Diosito's piece, I remember, it was as if "Mi Corazón en Fuego y Mi

Plan de Fuga" didn't end on the page, as if the last stanza were an appeal to the reader to continue the poem in his own head and in his own hand. This is the kind of voice the Will and Edith Rosenberg Media Center for Journalistic Excellence in the Penal Arts champions and was built to champion further, or rather was built with the goal of championing. I still find Diosito's first sheaf of verse galvanizing, despite what happened later, or more precisely what happened ninety minutes ago. I presented the poem in Volume I, Issue Eight ("Journeys") in the original Spanish with the faith and trust curious readers would perform the translation work themselves. (Folios are for plebes.) The Warden signs off on every issue, and I realized too late he doesn't speak Spanish either. He must have felt the same force of talent, must have intuited its power despite the pedestrian hurdle of fluency. His editorial note read, I remember, "More like this. Ups the otherness, good for reaching across the aisle w/r/t $$$." If you'll indulge me, I'd like to reproduce a stanza from that first piece, courtesy of Google Translate:

At the magic hour we will meet.
I in yellow, rising
like the phoenix, you
in white the exterminating angel.
Coming from unnamed roads,
coming from the southwest
with bolt cutters.

On one level, Diosito's intended reading is, I suppose, literally prophetic. But on another, deeper level, it is also figuratively prophetic. For how can one ignore the renaissance of the Latin

American "narco-ode" in Juárez, in San Diego, in Cozumel? Is not the work's literary influence the only criterion against which it can be judged and should be judged? Like Pound's *Cathay,* the words shed their obfuscating "meaning" for a libertine clarity. The world could use a few more Diositos.

Fox News Live at 5 reports the poet and his two (or possibly three) associates are still at large. Roadblocks have been erected at all major and rural points of egress.

And so Diosito escapes to Nueva York while I type this self-less auto-panegyric from the confines of the Media Center, which will most assuredly become my tomb. If I allow a momentary digression, I am flattered by the Kickstarter campaign to print and publish this blog post in luxe leather-bound editions. My flattery only deepens with the knowledge these collector's items are to be produced by Samuel Edmundson Jr., the artisanal bookbinder of Bozeman, Montana, with a twenty-thousand-square-foot work-shop and MacArthur "Genius Grant" to his name. Journalistic ethics prevent me from linking to this fundraising campaign—at 55 percent of its goal after one hour!—not to mention the imper-meable rules a work of literature abides by vis-à-vis merchandis-ing. Still: flattered.

A word on the merchandising. Though many products and services bear the mark of *The Holding Pen,* yours truly has never sought restitution for even a thin slice of what I imagine to be a very large pie. There's the O'Bastardface Triple Stout at cel-ebrated Danish beerhall Tørst, in Brooklyn; a limited-edition Lu-cite slipcase for issues one through ten, designed by Tom Dixon and available exclusively at Opening Ceremony; jumpsuits in or-ange colorways by Osh Kosh Black Label; "Westbrook Poppers" at TGIF locations along the northeast corridor; the Moleskine, naturally; and room 213 of the Ace Hotel Bronx, featuring a custom wallpaper of *Holding Pen* covers and contributors' mug shots. (I'm told the more licentious residents gyrate against McNairy's wan expression, the moiré pattern contributing to his come-hither stare.) All that money goes straight to Warden Gertjens's discretionary fund, and as far as I am concerned, it's just as well. I am not a marketer. I am a man of letters.

Which is not to say I'm infallible, or that it was an easy road to hoe, as it were. Was *The Holding Pen* a success from its very first issue? Your comments say "Yes" and "Fuck yes" and in one case a confusing string of eggplant emoji. In truth, this august publication navigated storm-tossed waters and a mutinous crew to reach its present shores of literary Valhalla. In that fateful midsummer meeting with Warden Gertjens, he hadn't given much direction beyond a name and a four-week turnaround for the début issue. The ebullience I felt in his office, sitting in the wingback chair, I remember, soon turned to doubt and then succumbed to doubt's enabling cousin, outright terror. The doubt was nothing more than the feelings of inadequacy shared by all great men embarking upon a new project. The terror, on the other hand, was unique to my situation at Westbrook. How to cover a population whose criticism arrived "knives out"? To be clear, I take no issue with the debate over the journalist's intention and execution—such give-and-take is the very meat and gristle of the profession. Rather, as I lay in bed that summer evening, unable to sleep, listening to the guttural rumble of long-haulers on I-105 bouncing off low cloud cover, I became fixated on the axiom "A little knowledge is a dangerous thing." The words floated in the blue air of night, dreamlike and oracular. How to explain the nuances of the journalist-subject relationship and its inevitable betrayals to a pugnacious subject like O'Bastardface? Janet Malcolm, hear my cry! Surely your reportage never bore such short-fuse scrutiny.

I tell you with complete disclosure those first few days were hell on the gastrointestinal routine, as bad as my first month at Westbrook. I would like to note the toilets are cemented to the rear wall and so face the cell gate and, by extension, anyone walking past. The toilets themselves are molded from a single shell (made in Taiwan) with a cold-water tap and sink basin on the left. While this arrangement dissuades furtiveness—you can still make toilet wine, with a bit of practice and patience—it takes getting used to. New fish might puff their chests, but we are all united in Week One bladder shyness, a personal Everest every man conquers on his own, or perhaps a universal Everest every man must conquer in his own way. All but the most fibrous among us knows this and must conquer it in this most public fashion, sometimes under the unblinking eyes of a screw like Wooderson just standing there, staring and drawling, in the voice of an incredulous, much put-upon blaxploitation star, a long and slow "Shiiiiiiiiiiiiiiiit . . ."

To those who suffer from a similar malady, I cannot stress enough the importance of visualization exercises. I have found solace and ameliorative release, for instance, imagining myself in the climax of the 1986 film *The Mission* as Academy Award winner Jeremy Irons going over the primeval waterfall on that makeshift crucifix. (I suppose all crucifixes are makeshift.) I am *père* Irons the fallen (and falling) missionary and also at the same time I am the rushing gallons of viscous river water, a kind of anthropomorphized, fecal tumult that can best be described as freeing. Incidentally, Appeals members know *The Mission* was Father Christopher's favorite film. McNairy's own method, which I hope doesn't breach a confidence in sharing with you: he travels in his mind's eye to Giants Stadium on game day, where he is seated in the upper bleachers amidst an ongoing triumphal roar by forty thousand screaming fans. He looks up and sees his own face splashed across the JumboTron, his bathroom session broadcast to and accompanied by fellow diehards chanting "Go! Go! Go!" McNairy reports a 100 percent success rate.

Is that a bullhorn? Are the state police here? A quick glance at the geo-tagged Instagrams shows that, yes, the state police installed themselves behind the GSSR's camp and are taking their sweet time strapping on the riot gear. My guess is they'll wait a bit before rushing the place: the media exposure demands the most meticulous and professional adherence to protocol.

We're all on display, one might argue—or I am arguing— including, unfortunately, the GSSR; it's their bullhorn I hear, held by none other than Ms. Rothschild's granddaughter. (I always suspected a fundraising connection between the group and the Bearnaise ladies' next of kin.) I can't remember her name, Tulip or Rose or Flora; I'd heard she was taking a gap year before Yale. Is she building wells in Papua New Guinea? Volunteering at the local Salvation Army? No. She's waving what looks like palo santo sticks and chanting, "He took my Nana's voice! Now let's take his!"

It's easy to find fault with the GSSR, but I do respect their passion. *The Holding Pen*'s splinter group of readers have published a half dozen manifestos on "intifada nostalgia," which garner audiences out of proportion to the merits, and I suppose I should be more troubled by the group's radicalization these past few months. The GSSR falsely alleges *The Holding Pen*'s best work was "its early stuff, when they were just doing it for themselves," and calls for an abrupt "dismantling of the scaffolding of the infrastructure of destructive affection," whatever that means. I admit even mentioning their activities and presence outside— and presence here, in these pages—taints the purity of this literary endeavor, and so I will do my best to ignore them.

I see my brief mention of O'Bastardface earlier has revived that old tempest. While I hope to avoid "feeding the trolls," as Marty Baron once advised, I shall address the vociferous lemmings blitzing the subreddits. Much has been made of how a convict serving eleven back-to-back life sentences raised a six-figure legal defense fund at a three-day Festival of the Juggalos in Duluth, Minnesota. Much has also been made of his coterie of movie producers and their quarterly "research" visits to West-brook, the fruits of which produced nearly a hundred cable-TV thrillers (*Dark Blackness*, *The Knife of Evil*, *Blood Passion*, *Fetal Vision*). Personal safety prevents me from besmirching the man here, but I remain skeptical of the endless font of gory detail O'Bastardface provides his flopsweated sycophants year in and year out. A close reading strains psychological verisimilitude: at age sixteen he favored hammers; at eighteen, frozen bananas. His sole remaining mystery, the only story he's yet to share with his rabid fan base, concerns the provenance of that Medusa-like face tattoo. Its rich greens and goldenrods had been inked in phases, indicating needlework by a professional (i.e., no stick-and-poke inside job). Because of the man's imposing height you first notice the two webbed feet on his pockmarked right jowl, then the vertiginous legs enjoined in a lithe torso, convex like a kidney bean, expanding into a large anuran visage—with a showman's grin and oversized eyes—and, traversing O'Bastardface's ruddy forehead, a spindly arm and four-fingered hand brandishing a top hat with Vegas élan. Everyone inside knows to divert your eyes in the hallways, in the yard, in the showers. Personally, I find O'Bastardface's tattoo a parenthetical levity to his otherwise brutal mien. (It should be noted face tattoos are fairly common, you have the Aryans' inked eyebrows, the Latin Kings' jawlined bumper-sticker phrases, the teardrops on everyone. O'Bastardface stood out because, well, his tattoo is a cartoon.) His witless defenders can flood the comment threads all they like. Their hero is likely disemboweling another inmate at this very moment, working his way through the riot like a salmon swimming upstream. Looking out the plexiglass window behind my desktop, it strikes me that he isn't attempting escape at all. This is O'Bastardface's Spring Break, he's "going wild." I only hope I can complete this testimonial before the psychopath breaks through my patchwork barricade.

Though in all honesty "psychopath" is not exactly correct. O'Bastardface used the term, a reflexive act of bravado common in Westbrook and exaggerated among new fish: "Oh, sure, son, I'm bipolar with violent tendencies." "Me? Respect, I got that impulse disorder; I got that oedipal complex with rage issues." (New fish were also known to butch up their rap sheets, trading drug sentences for vengeance-fueled homicides cribbed from the cinematic work of Denzel Washington.) This boastfulness went unchecked until twenty-three months ago, with the retirement of octogenarian prison shrink Dr. Gareth Edwards. After decades of halfhearted psychoanalysis, or possibly full-hearted and incompetent psychoanalysis—nobody aspires to land at a place like Westbrook—Dr. Edwards is gone but not forgotten, as they say. He left his Freudian thumbprint on the old timers' psyches, ask any of them about childhood and they'll ramble on about recovered memories of their father touching their penis, or their brother touching their penis, or their touching of their own penis, but, you know, aggressively. The rumor is Dr. Edwards retired to a Dutch Colonial fixer-upper in Old Chatham; I always saw him as a Bucks County type. Anyways, to return to the thrust of it, his successor was an eager Young Turk out of MIT's Comp Neuro program, combining the work of poststructuralist Jacques Lacan and network theorist Albert-László Barabasi. I tip my hat to the clever inmate who first deduced the good doctor's particular weakness: any appeal to his pride—"Doctor, you seemed to do so well with Rodriguez's OCD; he's finally on the path to balanced mental health"—and the young doctor couldn't help himself. "I'm glad to hear that you're taking this practice seriously, though to be fair to Mr. Rodriguez, it's nothing more than mild neuroticism, not the woefully over-diagnosed obsessive-compulsive disorder. Your friend's problems can be traced to the divorce of his parents during prepubescence." You can guess what followed. When virulent psychopathy was reduced to yawn-inducing "Baran webs of circumstantial hostility," everyone became a pussy. Well, almost everyone. The worst among us—O'Bastardface included—confounded the young doctor and escaped his progressive diagnoses, the maniacal peccadillos hiding in plain sight, as they say. These men interpreted this label-free label as a badge of pride around the flats. *I am beyond science! I am beyond language!* Or that's what they would have said if the circumstances of their psychoanalytic quandary did not preclude such self-knowledge. I for one remain thankful for the doctor's corrective influence elsewhere. Fact-checking *The Holding Pen*'s contributor bios was difficult enough: "I grew up hard on the streets of North Orlando. I was jacking cars by ten and icing snitches by twelve."

As if there weren't enough pressure to faithfully complete this final Editor's Letter, as if my editorial foxhole weren't already assailed by the shelling of naysayers and myopic old-guarders, it appears as though Betsy is en route, wending up the Taconic in what I believe is her roommate's Honda Civic and wearing her boyfriend's college sweatshirt—I'm told he's a PhD candidate in Cornell's school of rooftop agriculture. Betsy's polluting her Instagram stream with battings of eyelashes and poorly drawn peace signs. My readers and confidants, if you have any respect for my editorial project—nay, my life's work—you will ignore her meretricious "Who, me?" faces. And though I am not the type to dwell on the hypocrisy of others, New York State's texting and driving laws are quite stringent; the woman providing ample evidence of breaking such laws is the very same whose holier-than-thou position infests *Handcuffed* with lines like "The 240 residents of the Bearnaise—a bastion of old-world money on one of Manhattan's toniest blocks—had little reason to suspect their trusty doorman was a monster hiding in their midst. That is, until it was too late."

No, her arrival is most unwelcome, and I admit I do take a measure of solace in her inevitable delay by the crowd of upstate weekenders sharing the road, a mile-long centipede of Saabs and Audis inching along the parkway.

In response to her latest venomous GIF, let me defend myself and say: I love women.

A single rat darted across the hallway, just now, I caught a frantic movement as I glanced away from the computer, through the window of the Media Center. He was on the small side, with soft brown hair and the cautiousness of an emissary in hostile territory. Colonizer! I should have expected as much—rather, I do expect as much: the Media Center is just a few days old and it's only a matter of time before the rats move in. Everything gleamed at the dedication ceremony last month, I'd been invited to attend as window dressing for the photo ops. The Rosenberg kid—a towheaded alpha male sporting the tan of the permanently "summering"—spoke with casual eloquence at the ribbon cutting. He referred to his notes only in passing: "My father has been called a pillar of the community. He's been called a model citizen. But to me he will always just be Dad. The man who would play games of horse in our driveway for hours. The man who stayed up until midnight just to Skype during my Morgan Stanley internship in Tokyo. My father wasn't the type for greeting-card wisdom. But he did say something that I will never forget. At my Wharton graduation he took me aside and said, 'Live your life with a vision of what they'll put your name on after you die.' It could be a street, a park bench, the wing of an art museum, maybe . . . a presidential library? Ha ha. But I believe this place honors my father, and it honors my mother, and it honors their twin passions for rehabilitation and computer solitaire. I hope you incarcerated gentleman use this facility and someday become the pillars of your community."

The rat is inauspicious: whoever drove our little friend here must be getting close. For now the hallway has the fresh absence of a school corridor in summer, peaceful and unnatural. It will not last.

It's six p.m. Six p.m.! I'd lost track of time, incredibly enough. On any other day six p.m. would be religious services, continuing ed, anger management sessions, NA, AA, what have you. McNairy and I might donut if the screw on duty looked the other way, knotting a sheet over the bars for privacy, sliding a one-pound weight over the shaft of McNairy's dick, and working up to a rutting I always found refreshingly choleric. The cold cement plate against the buttocks operates as a choker might in a BDSM coupling, with the synesthetic bonus of semilegible indentations courtesy of the plate's raised MADE IN USA. (But, you know, backwards.) Donutting's very hot; I cannot recommend it enough.

It's incredible how open I've become inside. I remember my nervousness our first time; to be precise I wasn't nervous until the moment *of*, as it were, we were shuffling past a janitor closet after p.m. lineup and McNairy took cheeky advantage of my blind spot, tossing me in as one might toss his shirt into the hamper. Naturally my first thought was, here comes the stabbing. I'd been in ten or eleven weeks, I'd observed my surroundings, and though I am not a fearful man, I am a realist. If you'll excuse the gallows humor, I was surprised (in more than one sense) by the other kind of stabbing which followed. McNairy's rough approach was essential to remove my lifelong politesse, as I'll call it; he assured me I wouldn't enjoy it the first ten times as he "fucked the Catholic out of me." (Cries of apostasy went unacknowledged.) Afterward, in the humid quiet, McNairy took a pretend drag on a cigarette and said, "You know the three rules of anal sex?" I shrugged. He counted on the fingers of his right hand: "Location, location, location." Sweet McNairy! Even now I can see that slight discoloration at your navel, it hangs before me like a celestial burst of lusty melanin; how I yearn to kiss and lick it one more time, to bite your thick rope of stomach and fill my mouth with your sweat.

I see your #westbrookriot tweets, where I'm told donutting is popular in the Georgia and Arkansas institutions. Who knew?

I could write of my sentimental education for hours, but I must "look past the fence line," as Dr. Edwards would say, and return to my confession. Though my editorial stewardship has been called "revolutionary" (*The Nation*) and "reminiscent of early Gaultier" (*Vogue*), I still put my jumpsuit on one leg at a time. I prepared the inaugural issue of *The Holding Pen* in an unused vocational studies room, flailing without compass or rudder. Three or four days passed before the answer struck me with forehead-smacking clarity: I should copy someone else's work. But whose? *National Geographic* is a revered publication, and reverence is nothing if not pliable. I reasoned I could reshape it to fit my needs and hope for an afterglow of professionalism. (I should note that I hadn't yet actually read *National Geographic,* which speaks to the power of its brand.)

I visited the Westbrook library, though "library" isn't the right word, it was an alcove with a door, too small to even turn around in. Squat bookcases heaved with mass-market paperbacks and *Reader's Digest* omnibi. Good old Wilfred acted as our librarian, more in name than in function, often napping on a stool with his back to the decade-old PC resting on a card table. I was one of the only patrons, or anyway one of the only lenders, the others just wanted the computer time or one of the lawbooks for aspirational underlining. I must thank Wilfred for his generosity, he bent the rules regarding the number of loaned titles; a limit of twelve at a time, except for the Bible and the Koran—or rather I should say the Bible *or* the Koran—you could always append that to your call slip. (The Torah didn't see much use.) The first time Wilfred slipped an extra atop the pile, an old Pocket Books edition of Ambrose Bierce stories I'd wait-listed via interlibrary loan— Westbrook, New Horizons, a handful of Bergen County facilities,

Vassar—the first time he gave me the nod I felt an illicit charge in my veins. Of course, the screws counted during cell throws, but they chalked it up to special privileges. My collecting started in September, and within a month my cell was crowded with perilous towers circling the bed slab. And with those books—mostly library castoffs or rejected inheritances (hence all the *Reader's Digest*s)—the living histories of the objects themselves: tattooed with toilet-wine stains, Twombly-esque marginalia, and many, many pages stuck together. The towers got to be four feet, five feet tall. Screws would shake the bars without result, as if the stacks were possessed of an inner architecture outside of physics, outside of Westbrook law.

In my initial reconnaissance Wilfred said no other prison published a regular journal of arts and letters, as far as he knew. It was here that I began to understand the importance of the endeavor, if such a word can capture all that has since been unleashed and transformed and traduced. I admit now, hat in hand, I'd not originally planned anything more than the minimum required effort to satisfy Warden Gertjens—the minimum required effort being my personal preference for "going along to get along" inside. I'd seen time beat the enthusiasm out of even the sunniest inmate, it beats everything else out too. Incredible as it seems, I was asleep to my true self, asleep to the life of the artist. I've since drunk deeply from the cup of wisdom, replenished with TED Talks and *Tropic of Cancer*. You see, the artist stands alone. He stands alone from his people and at the same time among his people, not unlike the incarcerated man at once inside of and outside of society. You might argue because of this I have a *doubled* artistic temperament or at least a *concentrated* artistic temperament. I don't expect my critics or my lawyer or those blue-hairs' families to understand; they delineated small lives for themselves, they never sought the edge of the cliff.

Reader, you alone are my confessor and my ally; these words, my testament and my ablution.

In a way I have always sought the cliff's edge, be it the figurative cliff of artistic ambition or the literal cliff back in Trincomalee's north bay. Does it surprise the reader to learn I often hiked that mountain in my youth? I know how treacly it sounds, I wince as I type these words. If only those adolescent saunters were more original than simply gazing out at the refulgent waves. But there you have it. In my defense it was about the only thing to do in Trinco. Our lone soccer pitch had been annexed by a pack of mangy dogs, and bicycling was hazardous with the cordons of army trucks kicking up clouds of thick red-brown earth. When I wasn't tending to my studies with Father Christopher, I scaled the mountain and gazed out at those endless refulgent waves. Twice I saw Tamil tigers' skippers bearing south, their leaping bows hitting the water with shallow thunderclaps, their occupants standing defiant with to-do lists and purpose.

I remember one springtime weekday Father Christopher took me aside, wished me a blessed fourteenth birthday, and informed me play time was now considered idle time, and idleness was to be avoided at all costs. He needn't have said anything more, and in fact he didn't say anything more. I caught the conspiratorial look in his eye and knew I was being summoned to the hallowed local trade: catering to the whims of tourists. Today's visitors can pick from luxury all-inclusives huddled on the coast cheek by jowl and financed by the Chinese and the UAE and the Ian Schrager Company, but back in those days there was only the Palm and the

Ocean View, both owned by a Portuguese couple, the de Silvas, decent people with embarrassing accents.

Mr. and Mrs. de Silva reminisced often about the golden age, by which I took to mean the 1950s; I see now my golden age was just beginning. My teen years coincided with the drawdown of the conflict, plus I had the additional good fortune to be born Dutch Burgher: part of the local clerisy and, when it came to the separatists, neither here nor there. As any ethnographer of the subcontinent will tell you, I was bred to sniff out opportunities where others detect moral compromise. The tigers stapled people to the roads, President Rajapaksa volleyed grenades into the camps, and I sought my fortune. Before you judge me, wasn't it your Thomas Jefferson who said a country needs destroyers and rebuilders? Well, the destroyers performed admirably; now it was my turn.

The tapestry of progress is threaded with capitalism, or so the Hilton Hotels advance man said, and I was his servant at the loom. A charming Brit with patrician manners, he installed himself in the Palm's honeymoon villa and perched on the same barstool every evening with a sheaf of paperwork, sipping birdbath negronis and half watching the European children play with a lifesize set of checkers on the beach. I wish I could tell you what it was about me that first drew his attention. Perhaps he could sense my industriousness and moral flexibility in the way I swept the fallen palm fronds from the hotel's walkways. Or maybe Father Christopher's Francophilia had instilled a Continental bearing in my demeanor, setting me apart from the other groundskeepers. Whatever the reason, it brought the hand of fate to rest on my shoulder, ask if I had a moment. I remember it now: the hand of fate was quite pale, with blond hair on the knuckles and a pinky ring from a magical land named "Eton."

The Hilton Hotels advance man possessed the ease and bluntness of the born salesman, and in short order he'd prized my biography out of me, my biography and my half-formed aspirations, though in truth half is being generous. By then I'd already put in three years with the de Silvas, and he was the first person to ask me what I thought about anything of consequence, the first person to see me as capable of great things. I was wholly receptive to his need for the swiftest paths through Trinco's jungle of bureaucracy in securing commercial zoning permits on beachfront property which may or may not have been assigned to tsunami-relief housing. In this case the housing did exist and was in use, but its inhabitants—tigers' widows and/or magistrates' mistresses—were an easily displaced lot, nothing a few official-looking mailers and borrowed army uniforms couldn't solve.

Additionally, the Hilton Hotels advance man needed to know the respectful amounts of the many remunerative incentives for said magistrates, explaining that onetime bribes do little to cement the blood-oath trust required for large-scale development projects: "We're in this for the long haul, my boy." I brought on my friends Rajit and Georgy to assist in the delivery of these remunerations, the schedule of which was entirely my purview and, I must say, a source of pride. I'd entered management.

Speaking of trust, I knew I'd have to assure the Hilton Hotels advance man of his decision to work with a go-between such as myself. I introduced him to the Colombo municipal official who, during tea service at the Galle Face and arrack at the Captain, verified the magistrate was indeed cutting through the red tape as promised. (As a fillip to the proceedings I had the Colombo municipal official lament the absence of scrambled-egg breakfasts and American beer at the Palm and the Ocean View, amenities the Hilton Hotels advance man's Hilton Hotel would bring to Trinco.)

The Hilton Hotels advance man also stressed the importance of a "work-life balance," a strange term that caught on my tongue. He all but demanded three-day sojourns to Colombo, providing a list of recommended nightclubs and brothels. (Grand Opening had and might still have the best lunch buffet.) Rajit and I would freeze in the overnight train's first-class cabin under an industrial A/C unit, watching it drip onto the mounted color TV and taking bets when it would short out.

We had no illusions, we knew everyone saw us as slow-gaited upcountry folk, but any embarrassment on our part was subsumed by the general jubilation of the weekender on payday, as well as the specific jubilation of the weekender spending his payday on prostitutes. Which is not to say I was a total spendthrift: for that I must credit Father Christopher's financial acumen. While Rajit blew his earnings, I socked 60 percent in an HSBC online savings account recommended by the Hilton Hotels advance man. My needs were modest (and still are, really). I slept in one of the nondescript guard huts lining the Nilaveli Beach—tourists confused them for lifeguard stations, a joke that never failed to get a laugh with the women at Grand Opening—and entertained myself with the English-language books discarded by tourists: Nora Roberts, Patrick O'Brian, Jack Welch. After slogging through the classics at school this was something of a revelation. Though if I'm to be precise, my reading of the classics was done aloud, in fulfillment of my duties as Father Christopher's aide-de-camp, and not entirely for myself, as it were. The man's failing eyesight and the alcoholic handicap of the local optometrist meant daily recitations of favorite novels and philosophical tracts, the two of us sitting in teak rocking chairs and facing the bustling town square, now and then pausing to wave off the same three beggars. While I don't regret my time with Father Christopher, I do wish we'd ended our sessions before five p.m., when the nursing school on the east side discharged its comely students. My hometown abstinence in those days was most certainly buttressed by the emasculating display of reading Proust to the town's living symbol of fervent rectitude. A word on the books themselves: I figured Father Christopher's taste had less to do with the sonorousness of the French language or the existentialism of its literature—which, I later appreciated, swaddled the frazzled intellects of the wartorn country in a blanket of individualist redress—no, I assumed Father Christopher loved the French because they were one of the few European countries to never bother colonizing us.

One day, after yet another slog through *Temps perdu*, Father Christopher asked how the work was going. He said it just like that, or in an approximate Sinhalese idiom. I was impressed as much by his attempt at modern colloquy as I was at his interest in my perspective on my own life. I relayed all of the horizon-broadening tasks I was doing for the Hilton Hotels advance man, plus a bowdlerized version of my Colombo visits. His response, thinking about it now, may have been the most instrumental reply of those formative years: "To what end?" After which he stood and entered his house to go to bed.

To what end, indeed. I'd seen the Hilton Hotels marketing literature: as impressive as the concierges looked, their jobs and their lives would still be inexorably tied to Trinco's provincialism. If I may borrow a phrase by the irritating members of Westbrook's NA community, I'd seen the light.

As for the work itself, it was Father Christopher who instilled the strong Jesuit values necessary to arrive at my present station. Sure, there were others jockeying for position within the growing black markets and gray markets circling the hotel developments. I was twice as industrious, twice as charming, and twice as willing to do what was needed. My reputation spread and brought continual work—or rather I should say constant work, paid out handsomely in US dollars. And so it was that in my eighteenth year on this planet, after a year of self-cultivation and increasing net worth, I discovered the truth in what the Hilton Hotels advance man had once slurred after his ninth finger of scotch: in times of national upheaval, a young man can go far.

I realize I've been over-salting the meal, as it were, with all these rose-colored memories. If only McNairy could see me now, waxing nostalgic about the motherland! In these final moments my mind races toward the earliest moments, toward a psychological safety net, when in fact I must contend with my present situation head-on, as it were. Readers demand *an official accounting of events.* I hope you'll forgive these venial digressions, I know I must earn that forgiveness with candor and a laying out of the facts. Perhaps I should begin with the synapse-exploding, bowel-shaking artistic revelations I felt assembling that triumphant first issue.

Crucial to these revelations were the dusty books Wilfred pulled out of a rat-shit-freckled pile in the library, in addition to the handful of (ultimately fruitless) *National Geographic* back issues: *The Trial* by Franz Kafka, a Norton critical edition of the Reverend Dr. Martin Luther King Jr.'s *Letter from a Birmingham Jail*, the prison diaries of Nelson Mandela, and, just for fun, a pinup mag from the 1960s in what collectors would call "poor" condition. These texts changed my life, I read them and reread them and then forgot who said what in which book and read them again. Kafka, MLK, Mandela—the faces on my Mount Rushmore and the names printed in invisible ink above *The Holding Pen*'s masthead.

I didn't read *The Trial* in the traditional sense, I remember I found the narrator quite boring. No, I read it *spiritually*. Josef is my penal spirit animal, my incarcerated brother-from-another-warden. And, yes, I'm sure everyone inside claims he "gets" Kafka, but not like I do. Even now, as I type these words from the dubiously fortified Media Center, I feel the Czech's deep-set stare traveling over the astral expanse and drilling through my frontal cortex into the recesses of my lizard brain. Fear, anger, hunger, lust, *Franz*. My copy of *The Trial* is a cheap paperback from 1974, the inside front cover graffitied by three rows of simple declaratives in lead and ink—"Donald read this," "Juice read this," "Mehki read this," and so on—which perhaps augmented its talismanic quality. Despite these names the book felt thrillingly sacred and thrillingly mine.

I should note this informal ledger wasn't limited to old Franz; every book was marked as such. And to answer the question on your tongue: Yes, nine or ten names tracked very closely with my own path through the library holdings; my treasures had been their treasures. I came to think of these men as fellow travelers through the same autodidact wilds; but, no, I do not care to identify them here. When I mentioned my phantom book club to Wilfred, he confirmed what you may already suspect. They were, to a man, all pedos.

* * *

I see my pile of Aeron chairs has settled a bit. A moment ago one dislodged and tumbled over, producing a rather effective jump-scare. I know I shouldn't worry about the strength of the barri-cade: I've done all I can with what was at hand. I've wedged the fallen chair into a bald spot between a footlocker and the door-frame. Looking at it afresh, I must tell you it is incredible that this loose collection of furniture is all that stands between life and death. I bow my head to these inanimate allies and hope they will exhibit solidarity and resolve when the time comes.

Returning to the books: future historians and hard-core fans might be interested to learn of my own reading habit, wherein I pluck an eyebrow or two and drop it between pages, deep in the spine. I did this constantly, McNairy found it unsettling and once asked, "What about the next guy who read the book?" In truth I had these readers in mind all along. I hoped for some geneticist several generations from now, paging through, discovering this skeleton key to my DNA, and reverse-engineering a second ex-istence like in the Spielberg entertainment. Which is what I told McNairy: this eyelash habit was symptomatic of a fear of death. He shook his head and asked if I'd ever considered the pages' likely contamination by the eyelashes, hair, and corporeal debris of a hundred others, producing a worrisome hybrid of aught-years felons who ultimately destroys his makers and wreaks havoc on my imagined future utopia? I had not considered this.

One lesson I've taken from old Franz, based on my limited ex-posure to his work: Stay away from the ladies. To be more precise, the ladies that come to you. A true gentleman does all the work, and even then he isn't likely to persevere, and that's all right: wanting occupies the febrile mind. I learned too late with that Janus-faced Betsy Pankhurst.

I remember our first meeting well. After a few flirtatiously terse letters introducing herself and the occasion for her writing—an assignment from the MFA course "Queer 'I' for the Straight Guy deBord: New Journalism, New Perspectives"—she drove up in her roommate's car on a cloudy Thursday in January. Though *The Holding Pen* was gaining popularity, my only visitor had been my appeals lawyer, a frighteningly obese man with the optimism of a climate scientist. Other prisons have modernized visitor's centers with half partitions and, it's rumored, board games (!), but Westbrook is still resolutely traditional, and the E Block visitor's center sports double-pane Perspex with telephones mounted on the right side. (An awkward setup for southpaws like myself.) The guards cleaned the receivers with Windex wipes between guests; even now the smell of clean windows triggers a tumescent sense memory. When Betsy sat down, I took her in as quickly as possible with only a brief glimpse toward her breasts: I am a gentleman, I was aware of this and also aware Betsy did not yet know this; she might have been at that very moment expecting a most lecherous stare. I rose to the challenge, as they say, a gentleman above all: the table helpfully disguised the sudden rush of blood. She was smartly dressed in a glowing white wool sweater with a Weimar bob accentuating her ears. Those ears! Their constellations of red dots, swollen from removing the earrings at check-in. I was filled with a mad wish to run my fingers over their fleshy hillocks; I could have done it for hours. She wasn't petite but appeared so with an affected scoliotic posture I recognized as the "Otto Dix look" promoted by child soldiers-cum-models in the season's glossy magazines. (I report this with authority, inside we obsessed over every donated *Purple Fashion*, *The Gentlewoman*, and *W*, experts in the style of the day: how to evince "no-makeup

makeup," the "secrets to landing that internship," whether the ass was "in" . . . We laughed at that one.) I didn't register it at the time, but I would treasure her tight, pallid skin, an almost deathly look, and therefore a constant reminder of death itself—paradoxically, a total turn-on.

I remember we'd not even had the chance to say hello before a fight erupted in the booth next to ours (my right, Betsy's left). There was first a man and a woman, then a second woman burst through the visitor's door and beelined for the first woman. The screws let it go on a bit, the sheer entertainment value was so high, and as the women scratched at each other's faces I noticed my neighbor casually pawing at his crotch. Then Sanderson, an old front-of-house screw with truly impressive eczema blooming across the desert scrub of his face, he stepped in and evicted the sparring ladies. Typical. The visitation room was populated by the sorriest lot you've ever seen, scab pickers and bus-station rejects all. If inside is the place where hope goes to die, the visitor's room is where hope goes to live in a persistent vegetative state.

Betsy was unnerved. I tried to lighten the mood, asked if she'd read any good books lately—a cliché move, yes, but also funny in retrospect, considering how *les belles lettres* have become the centrifugal force in our romantic and adversarial *pas de deux*. She pulled out a worn paperback stamped with the name of a Brooklyn secondhand shop, and in a mousy voice said it was some recent sensation, the memoir of a soldier who underwent gender reassignment surgery during a tour in Afghanistan, *Tanks for the Mammaries*; its story is likely familiar to readers with more catholic tastes. (Betsy had even read a few sentences to me before I stopped her, the author was too self-pitying.) Though Betsy revealed herself in time a bilious memoirist of the lowest order, a grad-school Judas for the ages, I warmed to her every remark. She told me about *The Holding Pen*'s "huge following" in the Braille community, "among sight-impaired and non-sight-impaired readers alike." Her voice grew stronger and more confident, I noticed, as I tried not to look at her breasts. She retrieved a small pad of paper and casually asked if I had a pen she could borrow, as if I could just slide it through the Perspex. I said I didn't have a pen, but they let us carry pocketknives, did she want to borrow one of those? She apologized and then apologized a second time, of course no, she wasn't thinking, how horrible. I found it somewhat comic; you have to keep a sense of humor in life, otherwise what's the point. I could see Betsy felt quite abashed. This created a silence so total, so public, I knew I would have to be the one to break it. She idly fingered a corner of notebook paper, creasing the edge into a triangle, until I said I could ask one of the COs to take one out of my commissary account. She smiled and nodded as I motioned to the screw posted at the door and explained my request. After a long glance at Betsy he said she'd have to keep it. I replied fine, not a problem, make it so, all the while feeling the sting of the institutional markup.

Suddenly I saw us as the vacationing couple, she demanding the upgrade to the seats with more legroom. Or strolling through SoHo, slowing her pace in front of Marc Jacobs. *Ha!* My laugh startled Betsy, for a second there was real confusion in her eyes. In that moment I wondered if my pique was Betsy's intention all along, a small gift from the man who has nothing. It strikes me now there may have been an additional aspect to Betsy's machinations, a Day One test of my malleability and credulousness. Bravo, Ms. Pankhurst, bravo. I passed with flying colors, which is to say I failed myself. It's not enough to be under her thumb, one must volunteer to go under the wheel. I'm reminded of something the Hilton Hotels advance man once said: Sri Lankans were gluttons for punishment. How prophetic.

We must have radiated our mutual attraction, for Acosta appeared over her shoulder and said she'd had a cancellation if we wanted to squeeze in a quick portrait. Ho ho! This is moving along quite well, I thought. Acosta and her great eagle's nest of hair escorted Betsy over to the Annex of Memories while I exited, signed in, signed out, shackled up, received a quick pat-down, and met them through a separate door. I'm not sure how long the portrait studio had been in operation, but it was always Acosta's show, as it were, her side project and reward for a solid twenty on the job. I understand it's a reliable source of revenue and increasingly common at East Coast min-secs.

As soon as I entered the Annex—really just a wide corridor for the prison's odds and ends—I was immediately met by the sight of an African lakeshore with all manner of fauna dotting the landscape: ocelots, toucans, and an old silverback, defiant and sage. This lush vista was to be the fabric backdrop to our couple's portrait. If you'd told me at breakfast I would see a painting of a toucan that afternoon, I'd have replied, "No way, José." Acosta positioned us over an X mark on the floor and ran a couple test flashes from her tripod-mounted camera. (If Betsy noticed the tripod was bolted to the floor, she didn't let on.) Betsy stood in front of me like we were old lovers, she even pushed her ass against my right thigh. My cheeks went a deep crimson visible in the photograph. You might even mistake it for sunburn from a day on safari were it not for my jumpsuit and Betsy's winter wear. She said she would make this her profile pic; I replied that I was flattered. This seemed to be the response she sought. We were shooed away for the next family in line, whose patriarch thinned his eyes at Betsy.

When we retook our seats across the Perspex, I recall now experiencing a fugitive sensation, one I'd long thought dead and gone. A glance at the wall-mounted clock told me we had sixteen minutes remaining. I became aware of the limits of small time, that old bugaboo. It's a real killer inside, but still I welcomed it; small time was a cousin to that other rarity, sudden happiness. Of course, realizing as much tends to result in its dissolution, you may as well try to grasp the morning fog. I must have grinned at the thought, which Betsy would later embellish to—if I can remember the passage correctly—"the bone-chilling smile of the homicidal simpleton." Betsy asked about life inside, the usual tourist stuff; I replied with a few lines cribbed from Kafka and *Apocalypse Now.* She asked about the Bearnaise, which I admit caught me off guard, I hadn't expected such casual impertinence and, in any event, it's all ancient history. You would be proud to know I held my own: there was no need to go into it then, just as there's no need to go into it now; that wasn't and this isn't the appropriate venue. (Besides, that's what Wikipedia is for.)

To respond to all of the #FritzLives memorials flooding the Twitter streams, I will acknowledge yes, Betsy did profess her affection for the work of Fritz "Balls" McGennehey from the legendary Volume I, Issue Three ("Badlands"). If there were anyone whose prose reached water-cooler renown in our twelve-issue run, it would be Fritz. I regret ever signing off on his scabrous *roman à clef* of abuse and malfeasance at Exeter Prep, with its tabloid bait half masked by thin pseudonyms, a tale primed for tickling the erogenous zones of the body politic, and, even worse, Fritz went and killed himself like an utter moron. Page Six, Prison Radio,

"CSI: Miami," the rushed-to-production *dakimakura* "body pillow"—these sealed his reputation across all four quadrants, as movie marketers say. Fritz's fame hit its apex as *The Holding Pen*, qua literary journal, hit its nadir; that novella is truly a terrible piece of hackwork I included only because last October was a slow month. Had I known Fritz's plan I would have pulled "Youngin" and let the moron hang for no reason. Though I suppose if his plan had been disrupted he might never have punched his clock, as they say, continuing to live and toil in artistic obscurity, like all the true artists, honing his craft and eventually producing something worthy of *The Holding Pen* we know and love, not *The Holding Pen* he took a giant shit on with his awful novella. Reader, you know all this. What you may not know is that Fritz tried to kill himself several times before, always during lulls in the news cycle, before the AP wire closed for the day. (Eighty-three percent of Westbrook suicides occur on Sundays.) Lest you think Fritz a depressive case, a romantic case—exactly what he would want you to think, you should know; I hate to gossip but it must be said—he just couldn't master the hangman's noose, he kept falling to his cell floor in a blooper reel of self-abnegation. And to put to rest the rumors once and for all, no, the coroner did not find a short story folded into Fritz's rectum, that's hearsay—though in keeping with the depths to which the conniving bastard would sink—and so readers must disregard any new fiction bearing his name.

To his credit, the hangman's noose is a wily knot which demands practice. Wilfred once told me it is not uncommon for a spell of failed attempts to break out every decade or so as the inmate turnover takes with it this particular institutional knowledge. Every generation has to make its own mistakes: none of us are exempt, except maybe Wilfred, who replied yes, he does know how to make a hangman's noose; no, he's not going to tell you.

Happily, *The Holding Pen* remains a respected journal despite the blemish of the McGennehey affair. In the past two months alone I've been called to blurb new releases from venerable trade houses and university presses alike: *Boys Will Be Beuys: The Arboreal Penetration of Negative Space*, "A devastating monograph"; *River of Dawn*, "A devastating first novel by one of the premier voices of the French-Korean experience"; and *The Mathematician's Daughter's Diary*, "A devastating inquiry into the secrets buried between fathers and daughters, and the ineffable movements of the human heart." (I never finished that last one.)

I'd lost the thread there for a moment. My apologies; you know your mind takes the most circuitous paths inside. Someone should conduct MRIs on convicts to see if we're wired differently. Memories—that's where it really begins; every new fish and old-timer will tell you the same. You have your frame-worthy classics, maybe two or three dozen, the old reliables brightening your internal wattage. After a few months inside something in the archive breaks—it happens to all but the dimmest inmates—your endless inventory begins retrieving half images, unbidden, ghost traces of the nothing days of youth. An insomniac night debating whether the refrigerator from the Hell's Kitchen apartment opened from the left or the right; you're certain the one in the de Silvas' kitchen opened from the left; your hand crossed your body to grip the long, shallow arc of the handle, a gesture you repeated a million times—this you knew with certainty. But the Hell's Kitchen apartment? Maddening. And the rub was you couldn't share this with anyone, nobody wanted to hear it, it's worse than listening to someone recount last night's dream.

The very act of writing this down brings new memories forward. Or perhaps I should say new memories of the vexing struggle to piece together old memories. Around month ten I noticed an encroaching Technicolor filter, the hues richer, the soundtrack cleaner. I suspected my imagination and my sense of self-preservation were working hand in hand. I'd attempt to recall the moment in Montessori when Ms. Gunesekera asked each of us to recite our home address; it must have been an exercise in self-reliance, we were just out of the crib and already they're terrorizing us, Ms. Gunesekera comes to me and I freeze, I don't know the house number or the street—even worse, I don't understand these demarcations or what they signify. We never received any mail, and West Trinco didn't get street signs until the construction boom. I knew every second of my panic would only provoke suspicion from the teacher and students. Was it the same number as the previous student, plus one? I could manage that. Perhaps it's my birth date? That would be convenient. I decide to wing it, declaring, "Four, six, eight, eight, one, three, seven, six, five, two, four . . ." until Ms. Gunesekera's gentle smile twists in one corner and she asks me to stop and to be sure to ask Father Christopher that evening.

It's a well-trod story, one which never failed to charm the biddies at the Bearnaise, though now I wonder: Did I really wear faded blue overalls? Was this invention? Wasn't Ms. Gunesekera older? My recollection was interrupted by the higher mind, which, sensing the attempt to see it whole, assembled a self-defeating feint. At night I would spend hours debating these changes, measuring the revisionist damage, wrestling with the greased pig of memory. The unfortunate truth is this detective work fostered a recursive paranoia wherein the objects in question changed under such questioning. I knew better than to keep working at it. There was a real danger of losing my mental bearings; the Ourobouros of suspicion, once established, is enough to rend it all. I acknowledge this is how lesser men go insane.

On the subject of insane gestures, I might as well explain the facial scars. A few of you have noticed my fair appearance in newspaper photos and court renderings; in fact, I'd go so far as to say my skin was quite beautiful, moisturized and exfoliated thanks to a slew of Kiehl's products. There was an unspoken rule at the Bearnaise regarding frequent haircuts and daily applications of avocado-based emollients to face and hands. True, we doormen wore white gloves on the job, save for Summer Fridays. I interpreted my employers' desire for clean cuticles and unchapped knuckles as illustrative of a hospitality regimen ever more professional, ever more than merely skin-deep, as it were. Getting back to the scars, I'd read a BuzzFeed explainer on acclimating to prison life—"17 Ways to Protect Your Rep" or some such; I can't find a link, they must have updated the site's archive infrastructure— the article said cicatricial ornamentation acted as a kind of clubhouse password. The worse, the better. So my first day I used the two hours before p.m. meal to sharpen the end of my toothbrush across the cement wall. The low-grade plastic chipped off in powdery flakes and formed a small mound at my feet. I worried about breathing it in: surely the dust was toxic, they're always trying to kill you in the most banal ways, we kill each other with violence, I remember thinking; they kill us with banality. Anyway, I used the toothbrush to carve an ovoid loop over my cheeks and forehead in an approximation of the rushed gesture of a back-alley assailant. A few weeks later Lopez confirmed what I'd already began to suspect: most new fish enter the cafeteria with mosaics of cuts and welts, they'd all read the blog post, or at least heard its lessons. It was quite clever, I can see now, a brilliant piece of perennial click-bait and self-fulfilling prophecy. (Ed note: Betsy found the scars "super-hot," I remember, despite my portrait in her libelous tell-all as "spindly and lumpen.") No, everyone ignored the scars, they had their own, it didn't matter. McNairy said it was far weirder that I was Indian ("dots, not feathers"), or at least that's what everyone thought at first, in for killing my manager at the House of Tandoori. You don't get a lot of subcontinentals in the prison system, nobody knows Sri Lanka except as a Trivial Pursuit clue about tsunamis. I'd wager there are barely a dozen incarcerated Sinhalese across the entire country, charged with brief sentences for white-collar pettiness. Ethnically and historically I was quite unique—*am* quite unique—a gentleman Burgher among the pro-les. The Aryans didn't know what I was, but they were pretty sure they hated it; the blacks performed double-takes and made deri-sive popping sounds out of the sides of their mouths, which, to be fair, was their reply to everything; the Muslim brothers were a bit more knowledgeable, but I ignored them and they ignored me.

In truth this wasn't altogether different from my first year in my adopted country, meting out my savings, wandering Manhat-tan neighborhoods, absorbing, absorbing. I know how to adapt: it's a national trait. Sri Lankans have been ruled by the British, the Portuguese, the Dutch, maybe even the Swiss at some point. (I tend to believe the Brits stole our well-practiced habit of keeping calm and carrying on.) Many of you have asked about my "lost year," post-Trinco and pre-Bearnaise, and I tell you now nothing of consequence occurred in that time. How did I fill the days? I struggle to recall.

There were the weekly jaunts from the north end of the island to its southern tip, ambling down Broadway to the Irish bars dotting the seaport, each one competing for the distinction of the "oldest continually operating" establishment. Are there trade secrets to pouring a Guinness known only to seventh-generation barkeeps? Wasn't the entire point of America that it had no past? Its people certainly practiced expert denial of their own bifurcated sesquicentenary eruption, which Rajit's cousins brought up twice, possibly three times, during that interminable evening in Sunset Park.

In a total failure of a visit, Rajit snagged an emergency fare on a Qatari airline with the ostensible mission of visiting his expatriated relatives and an actual mission of seducing white women. Or, to be more precise, *a* white woman, a notch-on-the-bedpost that I would be hypocritical to begrudge the man. If you'll allow the brief indulgence, his first night stateside found us in some uncle's vinyl-clad single-family unit in the middle of nowhere, with a dozen Sri Lankans decrying reconstruction efforts "back home." The question on everyone's lips that evening, expressed with varying attempts at the mid-Atlantic accent: Would Chinese investment doom this once-in-a-generation opportunity for healing and for authentic national pride? I fumed silently from my position on the cat-scratched Naugahyde sofa, unfrozen fish cutlet in hand. Who were they to turn down money for the fatherland, no matter how many strings came attached? Who were they to be so derailed by the UN human-rights inquiry? From where I saw it then—from where I see it now—this was yet another turn of the wheel, yet another cycle of boom and bust. What was our country if not a succession of disasters? Rajit, seated cross-legged on the floor like a doting pubescent, mumbled assent to his family's casual madness while comparing local nightclubs' Yelp reviews and forwarding me his "faves for the night!!!!" It occurred to me then that Sri Lanka's the youngest ancient country on earth, wholly stunted, never more than a couple dozen years from its next destructive reset. The Indians, now they have continuity, however burdensome. They have the Buddha; we have . . . what? The sapling imported from the bodhi tree. Huzzah.

It's comical how my countrymen insist on long-term thinking in defiance of the face-slapping truth: catastrophe will bring you low soon enough, so live every day like it's your last.

Now, that's easy for me to write on this, my actual last day. But I would argue I've always lived this way, I've always "woken up this way." I challenge the record to find otherwise.

Speaking of lasts, that would be the last time I saw Rajit. I haven't thought about him much, and I hope he found the nightclub and the white woman he sought. I spun through the subway turnstile as an R train approached, he had to refill his MetroCard, you know how it is.

Where was I? Ah, yes, those first weeks inside. I was relieved when I earned a nickname; it seems in retrospect a real turning point, an end to the beginning (or the beginning of the end?). I give thanks to the Latin Kings for my Westbrook handle. Juan Pablo made a few inquiries, heard about the Bernaise blue-hairs, and found a parallel in Jessica Tandy and her trusty driver in that one eighties film. Then he simply rounded up from brown to black. So MF I became, and am, though of course I still publish under my Christian name. I will credit my minority status to a (relative) comfort inside, if not at present, obviously, then before. It was quite easy to move among the different groups at Westbrook, an outsider to all. Diosito, O'Bastardface, and the Mohammeds knew I was beholden to the written word and the written word alone.

I must also credit a lifelong talent for disarming strangers, well honed from those years in hospitality. Despite my one felonious transgression I remain, as McNairy has said, the very picture of innocuousness. While I've often felt my literary success the work of the fates operating my mouth and limbs like a marionette, my boyish appearance has afforded journalistic access closed off to most others.

I'd like to share one of my tricks for commissioning material for the first three issues (Volume I, Issue One ["A New Frontier"]; Volume I, Issue Two ["Geographies"]; and Volume I, Issue Three ["Badlands"]). Naturally, this proved challenging, convicts aren't inclined to devote free time to composing stories for an upstart literary project whose only recompense is three contributor's copies. Reactions spanned from "Fuck you say to me?" to the more polite "What the fuck you just say to me?" I learned to counter with a story from my time at the Bearnaise. I'd take my union break at one of the concrete benches lining Central Park West; it may have been Ms. Rothschild's, her family plaques dotted CPW like wind-tossed pollen. I found myself sharing the bench with an aggrieved parent and her mewling charge, a boy of five or six. I thought, Kid, we're all suffering, but he found it necessary to express this with full-force sobbing, a real capacious howl, his whole body slack. His mother wasn't hitting him or yelling, nothing like that; she was rooting through her leather tote for a Tupperware of Cheerios. No, these were the cries of a boy glimpsing for the first time how truly unfair life can be, and, worse yet, he had so many years of unfairness ahead. The race had just started for him—the rest of us can take comfort in numbness from overexposure—and he must have realized it was all rigged from the beginning. After five minutes of this, I entered a new headspace, somehow freer; the boy's concatenated sobbing became simple noise. I slid a hand over to his and pinched the fold of skin between the boy's thumb and index finger. He was really wailing now! The sound took on its fullest expression, it was primal, earthy, made to fill canyons. It was, I realize now, quite special to hear, and the expressions on the faces of passersby, expressions of "I can't believe it got worse," these were wonderful to see. His mother, oblivious, continued her search for Cheerios.

I'd tell the story and even the most grizzled hardcase would shake his head: Kids, man, what are you gonna do? This tactic was so successful, as longtime readers have noticed, we swiftly outgrew our initial page count. Two features became three, three became four, four became whole new sections—"Fiction," "Essays," "Lyric Memoir"—crowding out those front-of-book diversions I'd included as bait. I admit I'd been surprised by this respect for our readers' tastes; I had underestimated and I had misjudged, assuming these first *Holding Pen* readers preferred the lascivious tableaux of page four's connect-the-dots to the "dirty realist" short fiction. Yes, I know, I said as much in the Editor's Letter for Volume I, Issue Five ("Dreams"), and this is no time for repeating oneself.

Many of you know the early days of *The Holding Pen* and write asking of my own early days inside. They weren't altogether terrible. I'd made the mistake of having cash in my wallet at processing; it never made it to my commissary account. I wish I'd brought a fleece for the winter nights; I wish someone had told me that was even allowed. (Perhaps an update for that terrible BuzzFeed article?) But I adjusted. I adjusted and I acclimated. The volume inside Westbrook was new to me, or rather the sounds, not the volume: there were fewer of them. Six months passed before I realized I missed low-flying planes.

As for the volume, there was never true quiet—the prewar electrical system popped and buzzed without pattern or reason—but even the louder noises were manageable: a cry, a shout, barbells dropped. I would lie awake with ears tuned to the nocturnal soundtrack of E Block, its onanistic moans and the oneiric gasps rippling the surface; below, in the deeper water, the susurration of two hundred pairs of lungs; and, fifty-five inches away from me, O'Bastardface's reliable, percussive snoring. More than once I mistook my neighbor's breathing for someone in bed with me. On those nights I never dared to turn over and dispel the illusion, though it is true I've had fewer than four nights with a sleeping companion. (Colombo pros leave soon after end of session.)

It goes without saying I entered Westbrook unaffiliated and extremely vulnerable, but other new fish had it worse. One evening in the p.m.-meal slop line O'Bastardface walked up to a jaundiced fellow I'd nicknamed Summerteeth, probably a drugs charge in the hinterlands of Meth County, the poor guy had just enough time to put his game face on when O'Bastardface swept the man's legs out from under him and directed his head onto the metal railing, sending tray, plate, water cup, and stroganoff up to the heavens. I quickly darted my eyes to a fixed point on the ceiling and whistled some show tune. This routine was not personal, mind you. First-timers all hear the same thing: Pick a fight with the biggest guy, it shows hardness and earns respect. O'Bastardface was constantly under attack. Even a brain-damaged glance around the mess hall would identify the Irishman as the most outsize of the bunch, an ideal target for establishing credibility. It went on that way for months, Mc-

Nairy said. In the yard, at the library, didn't matter, young pups jumped him after a mumbled chest-flexing taunt, O'Bastardface sighing, responding in kind, the whole thing over with a swap or two. As far as we could tell, he didn't mind the arrangement: it kept him loose, mixed up the repertoire. But it was hell on the screws, they couldn't bear the tension, their hands at the ready, eyes on the new fish, eyes on O'Bastardface, eyes on the new fish, on and on. Eventually Kostas told O'Bastardface it would make everyone's life easier if he clocked the new fish at the outset. A welcome from the local panjandrum, as it were; the screws would look the other way. Incidentally, this new arrangement was how I first met the man: he turned from his first comer and relieved me with a light series of left hooks, my stroganoff also sent flying. Later I watched this scene play out for others, my role recast as the disinterested observer. Once you're in long enough it's all paint-by-numbers.

Poor Summerteeth. A handful of you have already guessed he was indeed the same man at the center of "Dispatched" from Volume I, Issue Three ("Badlands"). As with any gut-punching reportage, the genesis of the piece is itself an interesting story. Near the end of Sunday p.m. rec, as the late-September sky filled with clusters of migrating geese, we fell into single file for the count. White Mike and Steve lined up behind me like whistling shoplifters; the Aryans were never good at subtlety. White Mike leaned in and whispered, "Hey, MF, I'm your Deep Throat." I registered momentary confusion as well as momentary irritation—his goatee was scratching my neck—and began to outline my arrangement with my beloved McNairy, which I understood to be if not public knowledge then at least semipublic knowledge: we put up a bedsheet, what else could we be doing back there? We approached the faded blue metal doors, the CO's listless monotone growing louder, ". . . forty-seven, forty-eight, forty-nine . . ." We'd be split off into different directions in a minute or so. White Mike clarified: "No, Nixon's Deep Throat," to which I replied, "You mean Mark Felt?" He said, "Who the fuck is—never mind. Showers tomorrow, second shift. Bring a notebook."

Had this exchange occurred before *The Holding Pen,* I would have considered the request a fool's errand, a transparent scheme to lure me into who knows what. I can admit now that by Volume I, Issue Three ("Badlands") I'd come to recognize the higher calling of the Fourth Estate, heard it in my ear and felt it at my back. You can be sure this newfound confidence of the true believer was a novelty to an agnostic such as myself. The question was not whether I was going to follow up on White Mike's tip—how could I refuse?—but regarded the nature and content of the scoop. Without casting aspersions on the man, White Mike was never at the heart of political intrigue or sexual intrigue or even bureaucratic intrigue. The mashed potatoes were starchier than usual; perhaps White Mike stumbled upon a campaign to slowly poison us? No; he'd more likely hoard a smoking gun than fire it. Suffice to say my expectations were low.

Though I'm heartened by the essay's inclusion on so many J-school syllabi, I should articulate here, in my final moments, the writer's wont to embellish. "Dispatched" spends a good nine hundred words on the attack itself, whereas the whole thing was over in a matter of seconds. (I indulge myself a roomy word count as *un droit du seigneur.*) Prison hits are executed with a necessary economy of motion, not unlike a fast-food crew at rush hour. I'd arrived early and found a spot in the rear of the horseshoe-shaped room. It was an ideal vantage to record the most intimate details,

which I assure you were all faithfully transcribed—ignore the pro-
testations by Summerteeth's next of kin to Nancy Grace. I may
come clean, as it were, about one moment not transcribed nor
reported, a moment of both clarity and unsettling guilt. As Summerteeth first entered the shower, lured by what I would guess
were the flimsiest of promises, he saw me and my notebook; he
arched an eyebrow—he actually arched one of his eyebrows—I
remember, there was a kind of situational irony of such an intel-
ligent expression on so unintelligent a person walking into such
mortal danger. (Also, I was wearing my prison grays; he may have
registered the dissonance of the clothed in a nudity-standard environment.) On instinct I retreated three steps until my own back
was against the mildewed wall; at that moment Summerteeth had
the mark of death upon him, and sure enough White Mike and
Steve entered from behind. I recall the sound of his heel catch-
ing on the linoleum, the sound of gravity winning over muscle
control—it was the sound of the end for Summerteeth. White
Mike slipped four or five of those quarter-inch thick rubber bands
around the man's head and over his mouth, filling the air with
chalky dust and Summerteeth's low groans. The lights cut out for
a few seconds—I assumed this was planned—then I saw White
Mike and Steve pause while Summerteeth flopped about on the
grouty tile. This wasn't all that uncommon, the electric was noto-
riously spotty, the Warden said no amount of money could fix the
ancient wiring. Just last summer a fluke in D Block's circuits made
everything a good five percent brighter; it lasted maybe three
weeks, and old Ellis mistook this literal enlightenment for a figurative one. In no time he transformed into a proselytizing vulture,
swooping down on the carrion of philosophical debate: "That's
interesting what you're saying about Marx, but have you ever

considered the teachings of our Lord and Savior?" His lunchtime sermons drove us nuts until we learned to simply ignore him.

When the lights returned to the showers, White Mike and Steve resumed like two laborers performing their scutwork, with neither malice nor pleasure. After Summerteeth expired they nodded to each other and turned to me. I knew enough to pretend my pen could still write in the waterlogged notebook.

The next day White Mike and Steve interrupted my dinner: "How'd it look? Did it look good? We looked *hard*, didn't we?" I nodded, yes, yes, the hardest. To answer a question I've received dozens of times, I felt not the slightest hesitation about covering Summerteeth's demise, regardless of the outrage expressed by my left-leaning *Pen*sioners. Did I feel complicit in boosting White Mike's reputation? On the one hand, he didn't need it: word spread quickly. On the other, my coverage was at that time an untapped resource and White Mike its first speculator. (To play out the metaphor, I suppose that would make the Warden a kneecapped SEC.) In the weeks following the publication of "Dispatched," my concern grew in tandem with White Mike's effusiveness and the adulatory letters from that fateful grad student—more on him later, time willing—and I confess, at the risk of even greater public ignominy, a brief desire to rescind the article. What kind of precedent would I be setting? The submission process provoked enough anxiety.

I can see with the clarity of the newly sober that Volume I, Issue Three ("Badlands") is the fulcrum around which everything turned. Oh, to have remained undiscovered! I'd no idea how badly this would all turn out. I only knew, I remember, the deep intestinal shame, the cure for which was enforced isolation. Good news, then: I was in the right place for enforced isolation.

It was an easy ask of McNairy. He intuited these kinds of things. I remember the briefest mention about my rising and corrosive influence before he replied, "A fuck and a tussle, then the hole?" We waited until a.m. lineup, he gave me a shove, I responded in kind, we exchanged blows, the screws broke it up. If you've never had the pleasure of staging a fight with a loved one, I highly recommend it. I remember it as if it were yesterday, our mutual goal of really selling it to onlookers restrained by mutual affection, creating a brain-stem confusion over hurting the one you love. Around the fourth knock to the ribs I felt something much deeper, McNairy's unspoken concession to switch off higher-level thinking and really lay in, my endorphins flooding the senses: for two seconds this frisson of discovery brought genuine happiness. The Japanese call this *wabi-sabi*, though I may be mistaken.

It's the nature of these fights that the defendant receives the punishment—something to do with screws' reaction times. As Kostas walked me to solitary, it was all I could do to keep from whistling. I'd done one-day and two-day stints before, nothing too damaging. You want to avoid anything longer than that: you see it in the stoop-shouldered gait of the men who pull a ten—not even getting into the effects of a thirty-plus—they stand corroded and bent like hurricane-battered streetlights. I'd wagered three, maybe four days, just enough time to delay the production work-flow of Volume I, Issue Four ("Horizons"). (Yes, the one with the spot-gloss cover.) My hope, I remember now, was to convey to Warden Gertjens my unreliability, a mercurial nature ill-suited for the steady hands of a *Holding Pen* stewardship. Wilfred made it to tenth grade; maybe he could inherit the job.

Perhaps I should address that fateful grad student, since so many of you are asking for my side of the story. Ben Kraus, short for Benjamin and pronounced, I'm told, like the twentieth-century German philosopher. Ben Kraus, a shaggy-haired "All But Dissertation" academic who discovered Volume I, Issue Three ("Badlands"), in Westbrook's visitor's lounge during a research trip for a paper. (Something something "late capitalism," something something "institutional gesture.") He struck up a correspondence. I confess we found little in common. For two months I received weekly letters from the earnest young man—he preferred not to meet in person—his manic scribblings dense with rhetorical cul-de-sacs and page-long sentences. The truth is, even a boring letter will merit a response from an incarcerated recipient. I thought nothing of his breathless news that his four-thousand-word think-piece was to be published by ###, an upstart literary magazine from Bay Ridge, Brooklyn. Of course, I now know the publication quite well: they graciously send me the quarterly and its various sister projects. I gather it's an intimate operation, a clubhouse of logorrheic Harvard grads and rotating piles of interns. Kudos to them and their dedication to the written word! In these trying times I can think of no goal higher than the self-imposed edicts by these fun-size Sontags to reshape the worldview of each and every Brooklyn millennial. Kraus's article, I'm told, I remember, is in keeping with their general project. He valorized *The Holding Pen* as a landmark in "post-penal lit" (that lamentable phrase); McGennehey and Lopez were deemed New Voices You Can't Ignore, which some commenters interpreted as a subtle dig at the common diagnoses of schizophrenia among prison populations, but Kraus's naïveté trumps wit. His piece sported an unctuous dollop of white guilt, naturally, but in all fairness less than you'd think, and they even reprinted "Dispatched" and my first three "Reflections" columns through a syndication arrangement rubber-stamped by the Warden. If my Midwest and West Coast readers are unfamiliar with ###, I give it my strongest endorsement. Start with the most recent summer issue's "Salman on the Mount" and "The Pornography of Pornography." Great stuff.

I see activity's picked up on #westbrookriot. I apologize to my many fans that I cannot address all of your queries. Would that I had the time! A cruel reversal, I think, of the usual state of affairs inside, the garrote of fate tightening around my neck with every burst of clatter and darting shadow down the hall. Are they close? There's a trace of sulfur in the air. I dare not investigate: a great editor's curiosity is tempered by an equal measure of forbearance. I will continue, despite the distractions and the acid reflux to provide *an official accounting of the events, as they happened*.

To respond to 99ponda_babas's upvoted question in the Reddit AMA, I'll sidestep the more obvious differences and invoke the ritual of folding one's laundry. Quite often I'd return home from the Bearnaise utterly spent and further dejected by the midtown streets' sea of inhumanity, too tired to haul a weathered sack of soiled garments to the laundromat. When it became utterly necessary—a fortnight and a day to exhaust my stock of Uniqlo briefs—I would run this most onerous errand, staring at the tumbling, wet bricolage in the washer and, if I was lucky, entering something akin to a trance state. (I also entered something akin to a trance state during the hours of inactivity at the Bearnaise, and in truth for the entirety of July and August when its residents decamped for Martha's Vineyard and the Hamptons.)

Perhaps my fondest memory of the laundry ritual: pouring the Downy-scented haul onto my twin bed and separating the clothes into folded columns, an act, if I may be so grand, of rediscovering the molted shells of my former self. The I who purchased a baker's dozen of white tube socks from a fast-talking West African on Canal Street, the I who walked the sartorial tightrope of the mock turtleneck, and the I who endorsed the Hoboken outpost of the Hard Rock Cafe (also Canal Street). My Bearnaise livery, on the other hand, was always Martinized and heavily starched by a specialist in Turtle Bay, a paunchy Chinese man with yellowed fingers and a silent daughter managing the register. I mention this only to emphasize the alien nature of my "off-duty" attire—alien to myself, that is, the very person to whom it should be most familiar. When I unloaded the pile of clean and folded clothing onto my twin bed, a sensation came over me, I remember, of communing with someone who was not quite me and at the same time more me than anyone else.

Inside, of course, it's all yellow jumpsuits and gray jumpsuits. Before you let loose cries of hypocrisy, yes, it's true I worked laundry detail before that fateful transfer to my present epoch-defining post. But if I'm being honest—and I hope that if we can be anything with each other or to other, it's honest—we all know one's recreational pleasure becomes tainted when transmuted into paid labor, exsanguinated of the motivations behind simple "play." This is not to say laundry detail was a doleful enterprise. Sure, the summer months brought a noticeable spike in the human odors carried by the cotton-poly blends. But every now and then I would catch McNairy's unmistakable costume amid a new pile, and those shifts made it all worth it.

McNairy, as you've no doubt grasped, was a deep pragmatist with an almost monastic approach to material goods. His one concession to flair, then, was what Wilfred would call a "doozy": a single jumpsuit patchworked together from dozens of threadbare or otherwise ruined outfits he'd hoarded from his own time in laundry, which I remember he told me was about fourteen or fifteen months before my arrival to Westbrook. The final product was a magnificent quilt of lemon-colored madras. I had initially wondered why no one slashed it out of envy (or boredom, a more common motivation); the figurative abrasiveness of the place tended to become literal. For some reason McNairy and his costume were exempt. Now that I think about it, as WXHY Action News pans over the joyful chaos in B Block—despite one inmate's attempt to peg the strafing helicopter with Frisbee'd cafeteria trays—I don't think it's a stretch to say McNairy's jumpsuit possessed a talismanic quality inextricably bound to its wearer. Regarding which I can only speculate from within my decidedly biased viewpoint: at the very least let us agree McNairy's "just that kind of guy." If asked, he'd reply in his characteristically downplayed manner the jumpsuit is a nod to the back-pocket handkerchiefs of his dive-bar youth.

Perhaps it was the craftsmanship. As I said, even the rheumy-eyed Aryans on the base of the white-trash totem pole could appreciate the reinforced placket and back darts indicative of a high-quality garment. Perhaps it was the spirit of *e pluribus unum* the brothers and the Latin Kings so easily go in for. Or perhaps the respect accorded McNairy's jumpsuit was an externalized form of the respect accorded McNairy himself. He premiered the piece not long after my own editorial project, and while all of Westbrook soon clamored for inclusion in the pages of *The Holding Pen*—hitching their wagon to a rising star, as they say—McNairy stood conspicuously apart, adamant his own name and person never be mentioned. And though it causes me great pain to break such a covenant now, I hope McNairy, wherever he is—

be safe!—forgives my transgression and understands the extenuating circumstances under which I've done so and within which I type these, my final words. Thinking about him brings an ache to the solar plexus not unlike the feeling when the descending airplane first hits runway.

While everyone pleaded and cajoled for a piece of the literary spotlight, McNairy's contrarianism—and I feel as though I can speak for all of E Block on this point—demonstrated rare and personal honor. It was deeply American in that ineluctable way.

I see that even mentioning my beloved provokes an outpouring of sympathy on Facebook and Twitter. I also see the usual FAQs, which I may as well answer on the record, before my time is up. One of the most common questions—besides the fan favorite regarding the incarcerated's concupiscence and its unsanctioned satisfaction, with particular interest in the hows and whys of said release—one of the most common questions: Did I think *The Holding Pen* would become so influential and culture warping? In truth, I remember, no. Who could have? The sculptor chisels his marble: it may be another life study, it may be the very fundament of history. He does not know; he cannot know. The muse's banshee scream deafens him to all else.

Yes, there were clues, little bread crumbs through the forest of artifice to the castle of immortality. The joint report from McKinsey-Ogilvy citing *The Holding Pen* as a "key trend driver" in the Hong Kong luxury market. Wait—no, that was later. Volume I, Issue Seven ("The Patriarchy"). Before McKinsey-Ogilvy there was the forty-seven-minute disquisition on *The Holding Pen* by Senator Tim Wagner (R-ME), couched within a nine-hour filibuster excoriating federal entitlements. At one point I skimmed the transcript, but in truth I retained very little of the speech. Suffice to say Senator Wagner held up *The Holding Pen* as Exhibit A for the Democrats' bloated welfare state, a not entirely unpersuasive bit of rhetoric we later found germinated from his intern's poli-sci thesis. How this fresh-faced BYU alumnus stumbled upon Volume I, Issue Six ("Flora and Fauna"), I have no idea. I do know Maddow and Maher picked up the baton—almost simultaneously, if I recall correctly—and rallied around our humble institution. Maddow: "I've been a reader since the beginning. Very gutsy stuff." Maher: "Someone should tell the good senator it's better to pick straw men who don't shiv you in the shower." While the media interest blossomed and died within forty-eight hours—something about North Korea, something about kidnapped Miss South Korea—our site traffic steadied at a respectable new plateau. We'd broken through. When John Doe of Buttfuck, Kansas, thought of post-penal literary magazines, he thought of *us*.

Apologies for my brief absence. Wouldn't you know it, just when I was getting to the heart of the matter, to the white-hot center of this *official accounting of events, as they happened*, Devon the Pedo began banging on the hallway window of the Media Center. He's a boiled potato of a man, glistening with sweat and the wild-eyed exuberance of an adrenaline spike in full flush. He had stripped down to his underwear—or had been stripped down to his underwear—with blood caked over his mouth and chin. My first impression upon seeing him was of a large newborn. "Devon, my good man! How are you?" I asked, between the bass thumps of his fists on the glass and his legato chants of "Let me in let me in let me in let me in . . . ." I told him, "You look great"—he did, despite all—"but I'm afraid there's no room at the inn. Scoot." I pointed to the keyboard, coupled with what I hoped was a light-hearted bounce of the shoulders as if to say, "It's a living!" He continued his arrhythmic pounding and I was reminded of why I never liked the man, besides the pedophilia, or in addition to the pedophilia—which, if I'm being honest, isn't really a problem here, there wasn't any temptation or anything; if pressed I would say the man was simply a shithead. I flapped my hand to shoo him away. Devon glanced backward, possibly in response to something I didn't catch or couldn't hear, mumbled a generic invective, then signaled his leave with a phlegmatic gob loosed right into my line of sight. A class act, that Devon.

To return: the Wagner filibuster was merely the mainstreaming of our popularity. Coolhunters and tobacco marketers both know if you're going to get big, first you have to get the influencers: your Lego architects, your SXSW "experiential leads," your prop stylists for Japanese workwear zines. I direct new readers to "We Have All Killed the Widows," a rather thorough listserv of *Holding Pen* scholarship. The moderators claim with some degree of confidence two distinct and near-simultaneous first sightings of *The Holding Pen* in the cultural underground.

Last December a restaurant named Napkins opened in the Mission District of San Francisco, the newest addition to celebrity chef Frankie DiCredenza's growing empire. DiCredenza has the reputation for being as lax with his restaurants' decor as he is meticulous with his crudo. It would not surprise any of his many loyal fans to learn his first Michelin star (French Stuff, in London's Gravesend) was awarded only after fierce internal debate whether he even qualified: his plywood tables had been pulled from the refuse pile at a nearby wharf and gave the judges several splinters in their hindquarters. As for Napkins, the chef was dating a homeless teenager he'd found shooting up in the alley behind the restaurant; DiCredenza asked the young man to furnish the place for $800. Destiny pushed the doped-up kid into a nearby dumpster, and two weeks later Napkins opened to rapturous reviews about its duck à l'orange . . . and its curiously moving placemats. (That kid's name? You guessed it already: Grammy-nominee and MTV Music Video Award winner DJ G-G-G-Ghost!!!)

On the night of Napkins' soft opening, three thousand miles away at Brown University, a young graduate student was opening her mail. Anne-Elise Mulholland had pitched almost a dozen dissertation topics to her comp lit advisor, only to be rebuffed with the same excuse—the excuse heard by all the spritely academics in the world-historical moments before watershed scholarship: her thesis idea had already been investigated. Investigated, colonized, civilized, and overpopulated. Imagine young Mulholland's frustration, this constant running into the brick wall, bloodying her intellectual nose, as it were. Even her advisor, an old-guard Henry James scholar (yes, just Henry James) sympathetic to the woman's circumstances, vouchsafed a few alleyways of research: Might she wish to spend thirty months on the jingoistic effects of the Oxford comma in Scottish "bedside" novels of the 1880s? No, she might not. Of course we remember the contents of that fateful maildrop, we've all seen the "dramatic reenactment" on *60 Minutes*. Mulholland's cousin, a scrappy young Aryan National out of B Block, had sent her a copy of Volume I, Issue Three ("Badlands"), along with a letter Mulholland found, as usual, too prolix and racist to merit anything more than a cursory glance. But *The Holding Pen*: here was something new, she thought, she said later to Bob Simon, something vital and unexplored. In the

60 Minutes segment Mulholland began a slightly embarrassing reverie, invoking Cuban samizdat, the urophagic photography of Robert Mapplethorpe, and, I kid you not, "man's inhumanity to man." Let me be clear, I hold Mulholland and the good work she's done in the highest regard and intend merely a light ribbing. The rest of her narrative is well-known and not worth rehashing here when time is so clearly running out. (The novitiates and the curious should search the Smithsonian's site for her first bit of correspondence with Warden Gertjens, a real beauty, with phrases like "authenticity vogue" and "fresh claw marks across the commodity spectrum.") And for anyone who doubts her bona fides, I direct you to the acknowledgments section of Betsy Pankhurst's roorback of a publication and its sarcastic hat tip to the young scholar, noting Mulholland's professional reticence in response to Betsy's queries.

Here I must credit Warden Gertjens for his clear-sightedness. One evening he attended a Thiel Foundation fundraiser for sending tweens to intensive eight-month coding camps in northern Utah and found himself seated next to Benedict and Poopy Atherton, *the* power couple of all Dutchess County power couples. The Warden wasted no time, he's always been one to strike when the iron's hot: he pulled out a copy of *The Holding Pen* and said what he'd really like to do, what all the kids these days are asking for, is to bring his august print publication into the twenty-first century. The Athertons, who after five decades of marriage resembled identical twins, asked in unison, "Into the twenty-first century? What do you mean by that?" The Warden replied in hushed tones: "The Internet." All he needed was a $3 million endowment and *The Holding Pen* could be shared with the entire world. Thiel kicked in an additional million when he heard

Warden Gertjens intended to circumvent Albany for the funding, with the stipulation that English and Spanish copies of *Atlas Shrugged* be distributed to every inmate. And so we had our top-of-the-line, possibly overpriced content management system.

I don't need to tell you how instrumental going online has been for *The Holding Pen*. While I still hold my first and deepest love for our print product—Volume I, Issue 11 (*"Chacun à son goût"*) has nine paper stocks!—the site introduced us to nineteen million unique visitors and counting. The Warden told me we were starting to receive dozens of letters and hundreds of slush pile submissions—"I read a few of them," he said. "All terrible." He graciously passed along the notes of adulation and encouragement.

Beyond the metrics I began to appreciate our greater social influence. Commenters linked to our mentions in contemporary rap songs, where *The Holding Pen* had achieved meme status, be it A$AP Rocky ("Hold'er in the pen she do that trill shit / Off-White jumpsuit she gonna unzip"), D.R.A.M. ("I'm gonna post my love note inna Holding Pen / Cause you're a cutie / Take you to the mess hall for dinner / Cause I'm a foodie"), and Kanye West (". . . bring the club up to penal code / Grecian goddess wanna hold my pen and pen an ode / I bring her up VIP she want me unload, haynh?"). And let's not forget the striking image by French artist JR of Lopez's mug shot blown up to several hundred feet and plastered like wallpaper to San Francisco's Transamerica Pyramid, as part of the Levi's x JR x Blackstone Group collab.

Sure, the publication process was laborious at first. Writing out the daily posts in longhand while seated in a windowless office at the end of Times Square, delivering the pages to Kostas to give to Warden Gertjens's PA for transcription and uploading. The

Oberlin interns added images, A/B tested headlines, moderated comments, that sort of thing. (I'd brought them on after Volume I, Issue Five ["Dreams"]; our scale had made it necessary to enlist a dozen undergraduates to copyedit and track order fulfillment. I believe Westbrook received a small stipend from the university in exchange for the privilege.) I'm happy to report my column "Reflections" consistently ranks among the most-read posts.

As I think on it now, sitting in the Will and Edith Rosenberg Media Center for Journalistic Excellence in the Penal Arts, with the smoke filling the sky and the rhythmic klaxon blare down the hall, I admit to feeling a minor tremor in the otherwise unshakable confidence regarding my editorial stewardship. Perhaps it was Henry Kissinger who said, "Given the circumstances, I did my best." Could I have done more? Yes. Could I have been truer to my internal compass? Debatable. I know the true measure of my personal agency, as minute as that of my fellow incarcerated men the world over, and yet my masters are not penitential, or not exclusively penitential; indeed, the historical and social forces at my back are so strong I swear they take corporeal form: a hand on my shoulder, a whisper in my ear, and, when I glance backward at the metaphorical beach of life, one pair of footprints where the historical and social forces piggy-backed me through the hard times.

Dear reader, I know what you're thinking. The GSSR has gotten to me, I've "turned," in the parlance of spycraft. I swear to you now I brook no other interpretation of my success and, in the delicious phrasing of my younger fans, let me state clearly and definitively I "give zero fucks" about the GSSR.

Pop culture enthusiasts are no doubt familiar with their majordomo, the charismatic Bronwen Taylor, heir to a Toronto cardboard-packaging fortune and two-time X Games medalist in motocross freestyle. With his shoulder-length copper locks—professionally maintained by Quebec's most expensive stylist—his lacrosse player's physique, a retrograde philosophy of polyamory articulated in an infamous series of Snapchats, and his freakish run at last year's World Series of Poker, Bronwen Taylor has become a media darling for the TMZ and *VMan* set. As I understand it, his celebrity status and regular appearances in "Who Wore It Best?" has formed a protective extrajudicial membrane around his activities and, to an extent, the activities of the GSSR. If you'll recall the newsstand shootings in Hamburg, Lyon, and Antwerp on July second—assassinations in protest of the debossed cover of Volume I, Issue Nine ("Heritage")—Taylor's claim of responsibility for the killings was followed by their ceremonial naming of the fall guy, some wide-eyed Reed dropout with a martyr complex and, it goes without saying, the short straw. The poor bastard, I remember, was arraigned the very same day of Taylor's guest-host spot on *Live with Kelly and Ryan*, a guest-host spot which critics and fans agree was handled competently. (In one clip a blushing Selena Gomez complies with Taylor's request to touch his "righteous abs.")

I disavow wholly and definitively the actions and opinions of the GSSR. Let them bomb our printer's factory. Let them poison the gazpacho at our benefactors' gala. I will not be cowed by Taylor or his kind. I see them now behind the line of news vans in their slate-gray Jil Sander jumpsuits, unfurling what looks to be a protest banner the length of a school bus, indecipherable in the Instagram posts. *Ars longa, vita brevis,* plus some additional Latin nonsense?

At the risk of seeming uncouth, these *arrivistes* know nothing of art. The incarcerated man knows art, or at least is exposed to more art than the man outside; there are always theater troupes and grizzled troubadours working the circuit, chasing the easy high of altruism—people who consider the gift of song the greatest gift of all. They've worn down the grooves of their Johnny Cash records, they've heard the stories of South African prisoners' standing ovations for *Godot*. These actors long for such a performance, they crave it and they need it in a deep, almost embarrassing sense, they want one of the screws to openly weep at its apex, for the rest of us to whisper of it for years hence, to pass its wisdom to new fish in those somber tones familiar to anyone who's suffered an uncle reminisce about Studio 54 in the old days, before all the OD'ing. Not a week goes by without mandatory attendance at one of these execrable productions. These playwrights and musicians know their audience, they're stupid but they're not ignorant, every one of them knows we're the (way-) out-of-town preview. The material is often preworkshop and only recently post-table-read. To say nothing of the narrow breadth of its content, most often a chamber drama with a third-act revelation of long-buried incest; McNairy noted last August's production of *Beneath the Yellow Moon* alluded to a wartime rendezvous of siblings that somehow occurred a month after the brother was killed in Afghanistan. The "urban" plays are worse, tendentious affairs staged by a local group named the Spike Lee Joints and always a year behind in slang. After the fifth or sixth production I detected an unintended feedback loop of mediocrity, closed to the brain-tingle of *real* art. This void at the center of every performance became clearer with every performance; in a way I came to recognize art by its lacuna. Cineastes will recall a similar feeling among the French New Wave directors, whose films acted as an antidote to the studio dreck they'd reviewed as critics. Am I saying that I'm the Godard of contemporary prison literature? I'm not *not* saying it. Sitting here and typing these words as the violence thrums down the hall, with Death's arctic exhalations on the back of my neck, I can no longer pretend false modesty; the true fans of the *Holding Pen* expect no less. It is no longer the time for "being polite"; now is the time to "start getting real."

I fear I may have lost the thread of this *official accounting of events, as they happened*, as it were, and for that I apologize. When Kostas escorted me to solitary, when I took my seat on the cold cement that would service as chair and mattress, when Kostas slid the mint-green door shut and my neighbors whisper-shouted "Who dat?"—hoping for an acquaintance or someone with fresh gossip—I must admit to a swell of pride. Surely, I thought, I re-member, the Warden would get someone else to manage his pet project, someone who might better shoulder such responsibility. Wasn't there a rapist in A Block who'd earned two PhDs by cor-respondence? Or Yancey, the embezzler in C Block—his head is so far up the screws' asses he knows what they ate for breakfast.

The Warden bounced me after an hour and a half.

Incredible as it may sound, I now know with the benefit of hindsight, I hadn't *truly* absorbed prison life at that time. I do not consider myself naïve and did not consider myself so; rather, I prided myself—and pride myself—on going into every situa-tion with eyes open. How to say it? I knew the power dynamics of Westbrook, they were in the very air we breathed—heavy and sour in the flats, dehumidified and Glade-fresh in Times Square— but I hadn't *internalized* the power dynamics until that moment. Perhaps it was easier to feed my denial on the morsels of institu-tional routine, which is necessarily self-effacing: you can't take it personally. My mistake lay in misreading Westbrook's capricious meteorology. As Kostas slid the mint-green door open and gave a *You again?* look I had the sensation of standing before a tidal surge making landfall. We walked in silence to the E Block flats, Kostas swinging his club in a short counterclockwise loop—an end-of-shift habit, reliable as a poker tell. It was on that walk I came to realize my professed approach to life "with eyes open" had in fact hid a second, deeper set of eyes, eyes which had been closed until that day. The Warden wasn't going to let me stew in the hole, not when there was work to be done, and he certainly wasn't going to let a rufie rider or a dethroned Credit Suisse exec handicap his PR dreams. To even call what I had with the Warden a power dynamic was false. The phrase implies an exchange between two parties, and I had nothing to give.

No, to truly shirk my duties I would need to self-harm enough to land in medical, to reach what Dr. Edwards called Total Incapacitation and Bodily Surrender. Would it come to that anyway, by the hands of an aggrieved Westbrook contributor seeking retribution? I weighed the immediate threat of disobeying the Warden against the generalized threat of obeying him. It wasn't a moral calculus, more a moral arithmetic: my sense of self-preservation favored the specific. As you might expect, thoughts of safety and health are never far from the front of my mind, though there are of course the secondary, subcutaneous thoughts (McNairy, reputation) and, at a level just above inchoate nonsense, those tertiary, bone-deep thoughts (lust, anger). These are never fixed, mind you, they substitute positions with a frequency one might find worrisome or welcome, depending on the position substituted.

I fear the theme of regret will become central these last few hours. While nobody could have predicted the chain of events that led to our present situation, I am not above administering a mild scolding toward the Warden with respect to what happened after Volume I, Issue Six ("Flora and Fauna"). He was there for the first real bit of vituperative criticism—or, rather, there in spirit. Had the Warden intervened, I wonder if we might have avoided this terrible ordeal, this "teachable moment."

I had just put the issue to bed and was enjoying its brief afterglow. The next day I would begin the process anew with a kickoff call to the Oberlin interns. But first I took my daily constitutional about the yard, lazing through a 5K run-walk in 0.2K laps between the fence line, the outdoor gym, and the newer basketball court. Predawn storms had broken the dew point, creating a ripeness in the February air and a visual sharpness in the landscape: if I squinted I could just make out the interstate on the thin hump of land across the valley. As I hit my ambler's high on the twenty-second lap, rounding the basketball court and the Brotherhood's chess matches—stoic affairs with whole minutes of thoughtful chin scratching—one of the Hispanics broke from the deadweight station and stabbed me. A quick pull to the love handles with, by the initial feel, a whittled-down pen cylinder. Later one of the nurses would inform me the injury would have been severe had the wily assailant practiced the pinball-pull of twisting his wrist upon removal. Not a shivving out of anger, then. On my way to the ground I clutched the wound and exclaimed, "Good God, I've been stabbed!" It wasn't too far from the spot where good old Lopez was himself shivved; I suppose everything here becomes a pattern if you're in long enough. I felt the first rivulets of warm blood run over my fingers and onto the softhewn runner's trail. As was custom, most of the bystanders let me be. The Brothers noted their positions, folded up their boards, and moved to the picnic benches. The men at the weights continued their reps. Then a figure appeared, blotting out the sun, and dropped something onto my face. I recognized the smell and feel of the new seventy-pound paper stock—Volume I, Issue Five ("Dreams")—and turned my head to let it slip to the ground, I remember, taking a moment to silently compliment our new printer, a century-old family operation out of Iceland. The figure crouched down. I saw Diosito, his gold crucifix tickling my forehead and, as he peered closer, my nostrils. I unconsciously inhaled and hoovered the edge of the crucifix into my nose, along with the odor of the sweat-soaked weight bench a few feet away. One of Diosito's lieutenants remained standing to his left, I had seen the man around but couldn't recall his name; both sported a constellation of neck tattoos. In a creepy bit of stagecraft Diosito remained silent while the other man spoke. "Eh, *papi*, why nothing on the Kings in your little book? The Latin American voice isn't valid or something?" I started to reply but he continued. "Did you know Diosito's niece's boyfriend is a gardener for Luis Guzmán? Or is that not interesting to you?" My mind flashed back to the half-hour sensitivity training at the Bearnaise, and I said, I remember, "Gentlemen, I hear you. I hear you and I respect you. But what do you want me to do? A folio edition or some—"At this point Diosito grabbed my face and delivered what I believe is called the little butterfly, a rather painful cleaving of the lower lip with a vertical incision at its center. The shock of it left me with a rather stupid expression on my face, utterly unprofessional despite the pain—Max Perkins, give me strength!—I may have said "*Huevos noches*" before I passed out. I came to in medical with Dr. Edwards's successor hovering beside me; it was clear he'd been instructed by the Warden to closely monitor my recovery. God, I loved medical, it was my favorite room in Westbrook (before the completion of the Media Center). First, the lighting. There was a softness to the air absent everywhere else inside, they hadn't yet switched the old bulbs for the sterile CLFs, perhaps Administration simply forgot. Second, and this is not trivial, the on-duty nurse's desk could be viewed from any of the recovery beds through a four-by-eight-foot plate-glass window separating the two rooms—the nurse herself was nothing to speak of, an old Greek hag who nobody had ever, ever seen rise from her chair—but her desk! She was addicted to those Facebook games which incorporated the latest celebrities into arcade classics: you know, the Oscar nominees rendered as Tetris blocks, or the G8 leaders recast as Mario Kart drivers. I cannot explain why this fascinated me so. But I would strain my neck for hours to glimpse the nurse's desktop and her equally insatiable appetite for such entertainment. Perhaps, now that I think of it, there was something nostalgic about those games, nostalgic and at the same time informative. Whatever the reason, I took joy in watching the heads of Michael Caine and Amanda Seyfried tumble in an endless pixelated waterfall.

I was returned to my cell that evening, my convalescing lip protruded and pursed in the gesture of a kiss, an expression that earned catcalls from pretty much everyone in E Block ("MF got Botox! The better to kiss Gerty's ass with!"). As for the laceration on my left side, it was nothing more than a lingering sensitivity and a few days of wine-dark urine. Diosito intended to scare me, nothing more, and in many ways the most unnerving aspect of the entire experience was the tickle of his crucifix in my nostrils.

Naturally I included the Latin Kings' submissions in subsequent issues. I instructed the Oberlin interns to fast-track anything from Diosito, Manuel García, Juan García, Martin O'Valle, or any of their associates, and I felt and still feel (for the most part) this was a worthy compromise. Nothing stays pure forever, and at least we remained advertising-free. (The Warden had brought that up around Volume I, Issue Ten ["Paradise"], there was intense interest, cigarette companies mostly, but the board of directors forbade it.)

There was a loud smash against the exterior windows just a moment ago. A bird? People breaking *in*? No, that's too rich, even for my blood—ah, I see. According to Twitter it was a slingshot iPhone, sent with an excessive velocity by the Appeals. My fans, my true fellowship, I hear you! You have been there from the beginning, and it brings a tear to my eye and a catch in my throat to have you here at the end. My feed is rife with #solidarityselfies, hundreds of earnest readers sporting pins of split black ribbon, apparently the official protest accessory for the riot and/or preservation of the legacy of *The Holding Pen*. (It's unclear.) At the risk of "advertorial," the pins are just $2 at the Appeals' merch table.

My friends and allies, feel free to volley as many smartphones as you can spare, perhaps one will crash through, though it's not likely, I tried the windows with a few iMacs myself.

There, again! Another smashed phone. It is the sound of protest, a percussive accompaniment to your improvised negro spirituals ("Oogum Boogum in the Wheat," "Someday Parole's Gonna Come"). I am emboldened. I can see from WBCS's footage the detritus of several phones around the perimeter of E Block and the Media Center.

It appears as though the streetwear label Supreme is shooting a lookbook out there as well; @fre5hpre55ed and @drmarbles tell me the label is quite savvy. I direct the reader to their Instagram feed: one model is reading a vintage *Boy Scout Handbook* in front of the burning A Block, another is staring into the middle distance and chewing gum with bovine exactitude, and a third young man is standing just behind the WXHY reporter, mouthing along to the woman's reports in near-perfect pantomime. Good for them, I suppose.

The WXHY reporter's oval face and heavy stage makeup reminds me of Betsy, I can't help it and I wish it were otherwise. She has the same high forehead and, well, now that I recall, Betsy's forehead is quite different, the reporter looks nothing like her, people are always reminiscent of someone until you really look. The last time I saw Betsy—in person, that is—it was quite a memorable afternoon, which I credit to a revisionist somberness— revised in the light of her betrayal—and not because it happened to be my last sexual encounter with a woman. The Warden inferred all he needed from spying Betsy's name on my visitors' carbons—since early January she'd visited every two weeks with clockwork precision—and he told me, with his repugnant Dutch grin, that I'd be receiving my visitors in A Block henceforth. He needn't have said anything more. A Block housed the least violent offenders, a real milquetoast lot kept mostly separated from C, D, and E Blocks. A Block didn't need Perspex dividers; they even had a small room retrofitted for conjugal visits.

I should note before I commence with a well-earned erotic reverie that I do not wish to slander Betsy Pankhurst. I aim to rise above her own slander of me in providing my *official accounting of events, as they happened*. She may take to the morning shows and attempt to spin what I've shared here, but I am beholden only to you—to you and to the truth. Also, I will be dead by then.

The Warden relayed my good news on the first Thursday in March. I had three days to obsess over Betsy's visit, though my obsession was misdirected, or at best futile. To explain: for some reason I became fixated on her pubic hair, it filled my thoughts and dreams. I imagined, I remember, her hair silken from long baths, enriched by products with French names and imbued with botanicals, whatever botanicals are. A two-inch tuft better kempt and more loved, I daresay more respected, than anything in Westbrook. More than anything in life, really. Even starving African children, if they could see that treasured pubis—threaded by the evening light through A Block's cross-hatched windows, rising and falling with each breath—each and every child would say, "Keep your money, buy more botanicals, this is the bush of a goddess."

The visit began similar to the others she'd made; I'm not sure she even noticed our new arrangement, side by side at a plastic picnic table affixed to the ground. She launched into conversation by relaying her mother's good fortune, apparently Dr. Pankhurst—a respected veterinary radiologist with a midsize practice in Stamford—had been awarded *Field & Stream*'s top ranking in their annual "Best Doctors" issue. I watched as she talked and talked. There was an anecdote about a woman named Tiana, Betsy had seen her at security intake a few times and they'd become friendly—thinking about it now, it may have been Francisco's girl—and Betsy had invited Tiana to a dinner party she was hosting. Tiana showed up early with pigs in blankets and something else, I can't remember; the gist of the story is somebody stole pills from the medicine cabinet, Betsy and her two roommates confronted the guests over peach cobbler, there was a painful minute of silence with eyes on Tiana until one of the roommate's boyfriends admitted he'd swallowed all the Xanax because he "found you all so terribly boring." I chuckled to let Betsy know I was listening.

It was then Wooderson caught my eye: he gave the slightest nod to the left—well, *his* right, *my* left—and I intuited at once what was happening. "Listen," I told Betsy, "I believe this might be the only time we can do this, it's a lot to ask . . ." Here I should admit I will provide details only in counterpoint to what you may see or hear about in *Handcuffed*, as we both know I am and have always been a model of propriety, a model of restraint. It is also worth noting we had but ten minutes of privacy; Wooderson said they were backed up for the day. I instinctively cursed, thinking of those lax A Blockers' discourteous approach to time. Betsy mistook my umbrage for a minor act of rebellion against Wooderson himself and squeezed my hand as we crossed the threshold, as it were.

The room itself was nothing special, an old couch against the back wall, condom resting on one arm and a folding card table in the center. I dashed to the couch and tossed the cushions to pull out the folded bed frame underneath, only to discover the steel arms had locked shut with overuse, or perhaps misuse. Betsy helped me reset the cushions; it was then I realized we hadn't said anything, it was all understood. I see now this wasn't my golden opportunity, it was hers, she knew at once the material the occasion would provide. In any case we disrobed with alacrity and assumed the missionary position, I'm not sure why that one in particular, it was of course a total mistake, owing to a lump in the couch which pitched her lower back up and her pelvis down, such that I couldn't lower my own hips enough to enter and penetrate upward. I was like a child reaching up into a vending machine, the prized bag of chips just out of reach. Further complicating matters was the small Band-Aid just above the nipple of her left breast, I wanted to ask about it, I became obsessed with asking about it but knew this was not the time, and in truth I may have simply been allowing myself to get distracted. I was never one for focus when it was most demanded of me. Betsy made a circular motion with her index finger, we flipped over, she on top. I came. She did indeed have a wonderful pubis, perhaps the only authentic and beautiful part of Betsy Pankhurst. Certainly not her postcoital manner, a raising of the eyebrows implying all sorts of performance-related anxieties best not made explicit here. She pretended to look at her watch, dismounted, and did me the courtesy of tying off the condom. If memory serves, we left it on the card table.

That's it. What I summarized in one paragraph somehow merited nineteen pages in *Handcuffed*, and I swear if she'd voiced any complaints with respect to pleasure on her part I would have obliged however I could in the time allotted. I should also note there was no BDSM play and no crying out for Mother.

I do recall spying a curlicue of my own chest hair on her modest cleavage; it remained while she put her clothes back on, a companion for the walk back to her roommate's Honda Civic, back to her ivy-dressed campus, back to her apartment and its institutional fluorescents. (So much in common!) My follicular emissary would tickle her during Post-Colonial Lit seminars and cling for dear life during gin-fueled intercourse with the Cornell PhD candidate/fuck buddy.

I do remember our pillow talk, as it were; we were more efficient than I'd thought, or perhaps Wooderson was doing me a solid. I inquired about her studies, she demurred and said it wasn't very interesting. Betsy asked if anti-Semitism was a problem inside. There were a few White Nationalists, I replied, they beat or stabbed guys every now and then, but so did everyone else. Judaism seemed an affront equal to getting a "better" portion on Sloppy Joe Day. Besides, Steve bought his weed from the Muslim Brothers, which to my mind indicates a flexible orthodoxy, or at least a pragmatic one. Everyone adapts, is my point. It's a strength, the Hilton Hotels advance man told me, the world is always changing, you have to be ready for it. He said, and I'm paraphrasing, hardheadedness leads to zealotry, and zealots, besides making for the worst dinner-party conversationalists, choose conflict at their own expense.

Betsy was disappointed by my comments, I remember. She asked if McNairy was circumcised. I said what we do is private.

Many of you have been asking about hate crimes, and, yes, you'd hear the stories; there were stories about everything. Reports of p.m.-lineup shivs tended toward the dramatic: "It's gang retribution," "He disrespected him," "You put Dominicans and Puerto Ricans together, what do you expect?" I once overheard Kostas tell another screw it was a cyclical thing, like allergy season, which I'm inclined to believe.

That was the last time I saw Betsy in the flesh; the supposed halcyon days ended with a lumpy couch and a chat about skinheads. She was wearing a tweed skirt and an orange merino sweater, perhaps a vintage find, and black leggings, a pair of duck boots. Did she already have the book deal in hand? Was it all a ploy? Did I break through the icy exterior? I'll never know. The last thing she said to me, with lightness in her voice and an ominous insouciance: "Okay, then." With the clarity of impending death I can now grasp the full measure of my time with Betsy, the five visits, the seventeen letters, the frantic consummation. How she turned these meager scraps into a 480-page tell-all is a feat to rival the best reality TV. Though I've often thought of something she said in that first visit, which felt complimentary in the moment but has since taken on the gray shade of disappointment: "You're different than I thought you'd be."

In my remaining time, these precious minutes and—do I dare hope?—hours, I must not grant Betsy Pankhurst any more "screen time" than she's already wrested from this, the final issue. Though I will say it is not surprising to see the Cornell PhD candidate standing with Bronwen Taylor in protest, I recognize him from Katie Couric's prime-time interview. In the segment he's dressed in a box-fresh white button-down and jeans, holding Betsy's hand, possibly the most unnatural pose for two people on a couch. From the Ethan Allen decor I assume it was filmed in the living room of her thesis advisor's Tudor-style mansion. (Yes, we watch Katie Couric. No, it's not a sex thing. We respect her ease with interview subjects and her hardball approach.) I must question the Cornell PhD candidate's motives for joining the GSSR in light of what I surmise are very recent correctives to his assumptions vis-à-vis relationship exclusivity with Betsy Pankhurst. On the other hand, she does like her men radicalized. The GSSR's chants are indistinguishable online and drowned out by helicopters IRL; my guess is it's a supererogatory pop tune Taylor commissioned from a Jack Antonoff type. (A quick search on Spotify confirms my suspicion: "My Horizons, Your Dreams," by Miguel feat. Bronwen Taylor & Carly Rae Jepsen.) While I applaud their conviction, I wonder why the GSSR doesn't simply stop reading the publication, or divert their enthusiasm to one of the many also-rans that have debuted in the last six months. There's *Bars*, a rather impressive quarterly from Annandale, outside of Boston, which, to cite their website's About page, wishes "to apply a critical lens to the post-Foucauldian ([un]self)-imprisonment of the post-human"—likely a reference to Annandale's population's Fitbits, some start-up founder's tax write-off—"and demarcate an aesthetics apart from the farrago of so-called penal literature . . ." It goes on for another ten thousand words; you get the idea. As a brief aside, and to respond to all the tweets about bandwagon jumping, I truly and definitively do not mind such efforts, I look upon it with the respectful gaze of a friendly patrician—yes, even Annandale's forthcoming "symposia" with its corporate sponsors and facile programming ("Damien Echols & Fredric Jameson in Conversation"). Regarding such exegesis, however, my own principles are well established. In keeping with the tenets of the New Criticism, I reject the life of the author, or the life of the editor, as it were, and ask my readers to do the same. To be honest, I'm a little relieved to know I'll soon be dead and free of interference, however unintentional. At the risk of *lèse-majesté*, I hope Warden Gertjens is also dead, for this reason only.

Well, another reason. Though he and I spoke of it only once, the issue of editorial ownership remains a sticking point. The Warden, I remember now, likened me to a midwife and *The Holding Pen*, to extend the metaphor, Westbrook's offspring. We were reviewing my draft of the TOC for either Volume I, Issue Five ("Dreams"), or Volume I, Issue Six ("Flora and Fauna"), I can't remember which, at some point he leaned back in his Wegner chair and expounded upon the unique circumstances under which my so-called intellectual property had been manifest, specifically as the output of inmate work detail, which is of course subsidized by state and federal taxes. *The Holding Pen* is best thought of as an allodial fixture under Westbrook sovereignty, a self-enclosed, nebulous commonwealth. Furthermore, he added, as a consequence of a 1989 "civil death" statute in the penal code, the New York DOC regarded all writing produced by state prisoners as state property, just as a chair assembled in the woodshop belonged to the state. But it is not to the letter of the law that I appeal, rather its spirit, its *cri de coeur*, its "flavor savor."

I worry that I've gone thoroughly "off the rails," as it were, in my apologia. I've begun paging through the archives; it was Wilfred's idea to keep a set on a beautiful cherrywood bookshelf here in the Media Center, and the nostalgia brings a tear to my eye, I don't mind telling you. The closer we come to the end, the warmer the embrace of the past—and the greater the temptation to romanticize and misrepresent. We are inevitably nostalgic for our youth, though perhaps that's imprecise. Rather, it is our potential we miss, potential unfulfilled, or fulfilled by the wrong choices. Here I must take solace: regrets, I have none. Or, rather, I regret not living to see the publication of those unfulfilled *Holding Pen*s. Volume I, Issue Fourteen ("Feelings"). Volume I, Issue Fifteen ("Kiwi Watermelon"). The oversized fifth anniversary volume with Rizzoli. The page-a-day calendar with Andrews McMeel.

Ah, Volume I, Issue Seven ("The Patriarchy")! A stunning issue, time has only burnished its inner verities. A. F. Aguilar's "Cocina Muy Caliente," whose stanzas dance across the lips of Hispanic matriarchs everywhere, whose opening couplet is *the* bumper sticker of Cancún pedicabs—usurping the old standby "How's My Driving? Call 1-800-FUCK-OFF"—and whose repeating line *"Cocina! Cocina! ¿Donde está el viento?"* has become a call-and-response standard in the Sonoran EDM scene—thousands of ravers chanting *"Vientooooooooooooo"* on the breakdown with a pantomime kiss to the DJ . . . The poem is well on its way to folk-myth status. And Volume I, Issue Two ("Geographies"), *such* an improvement on our début. This is where we really "came into our own," excepting Lopez's lachrymose contribution, otherwise it's strong front-to-back, courtesy of a design rethink executed by Pentagram pro bono. Peter Beirut said they didn't change *The Holding Pen* so much as "allow it be what it was always meant to be."

I will not discuss Volume I, Issue Nine ("Heritage").

If WCBS's cameras can zoom in, it appears as though, yes, it's Miller, one of the screws from E Block, he's made a break for it through the west lawn. His uniform has been rent to rags, exposing numerous cuts and bruises; he's cradling his right arm; still, he should be happy to be alive, he must have been close to Times Square when this all started. Miller's one of the good ones, or at least not one of the bad ones, though not without his quirks. I remember it was my second week inside, I shuffled by the E Block station while he complained to another screw about pulling monitor duty—a six-hour shift in front of a bank of surveillance feeds, squinting to see if the grainy shapes cohere into activity that might be considered suspicious—Miller said, "Sometimes I imagine the cameras go deeper. They show the bones, the organs. No skin, no tattoos, no eyes. And not just them. The COs, too, just these piles of muscles and bones ambling from room to room." I wasn't surprised to hear this: prison was like a sensory deprivation chamber. In other ways prison was like a monastery, and in other ways prison wasn't a metaphor for anything.

Those first months are the hardest, don't let anyone fool you, your body and your mind refuse to adjust to the rhythms and limitations of prison life: first your bowels will not cooperate, then they cannot be stopped. You'll write letters to everyone you've ever met, then you'll have nothing to say. You'll take a morning jog and discover your ankles have shrunken overnight, sending you to the ground three times before you give up. Then a curious thing happens: the days go on, they flatten out, and in their accumulation mithridatize you to the poison of time. McNairy chalked this up to American resilience; Wilfred called it the awful mutability of man. Still, good to see Miller made it. I suspect many of his colleagues haven't fared so well.

It's become quite clammy in here, I must acknowledge the clamminess and the back-sweat, I'd never before considered the room temperature of my final day on earth. Someone has cut the A/C, and looking over the computer monitor and down the hallway I can see the first clouds of smoke, still quite thin, the visibility remains more than generous. The sulfurous tinge to the air is stronger, plus the smell of burnt tires, however improbable that may be. If I can hazard a brief expedition into the hallway, perhaps I can suss out just how much time I have left, how much time *we* have left.

Do I dare? Dismantling the barricade of Aeron chairs, footlockers, teacher's desk, and *Britannica*s might take eight or nine minutes, and less time to rebuild it (practice). The longer I wait, the more dangerous my expedition becomes.

I've returned. I do not exaggerate when I write my *esprit de corps* for you has magnified in the last fifteen minutes, it has magnified and it has multiplied. I needn't bore you about my desperate reconnoiter, especially when I have so much left to confess and impart in this, the final issue of *The Holding Pen*; suffice to say the riot proceeds apace. The fires in A and B Blocks hindered any escape through Central Booking, directing the truculent masses into C and D Blocks. I can only express my deepest hope for Mc-Nairy's safety. If there is a Westbrook after today, I will happily accede editorial control to my inamorato; he would make a capable steward of *The Holding Pen II: A New Beginning*. As I've said, I believe McNairy's *geist* touches every page, every word, every tittle. Have I mentioned his interest in the etymology of American axioms? Or, to be more specific, his interest in the etymology of American axioms he surmised to have originated with convicts: "You can't swing a dead cat in here without _____," "There's more than one way to skin a cat," a few others I'm forgetting, in all likelihood similarly feline in content.

If you'll forgive a moment of woolgathering, I remember our meet-cute, it happened, as they say, on a Tuesday. I was shuffling down the cafeteria line for p.m. meal, always a dispiriting endeavor: nothing says endless routine like passing a twelve-gallon tub of mayonnaise nestled behind the prep trays. In those early days I remember my foolish optimism regarding the pudding; this was before Wilfred informed me its bargain-basement viscosity had been responsible for at least one choking death. As was customary I kept my head on a swivel, taking everything in, silently chastising everyone's poor back-posture, row after row of men bent like supplicants. (Except for the Muslim Brothers, they sit erect with sphincters fully tightened.)

I felt eyes on me. Mind you, I was still on edge after that first bit with O'Bastardface, still quaking when the shower water hit my face. All to say I could feel the eyes on me before I could see the eyes on me, before I turned around and met them in kind. I was startled to encounter the friendly expression of a man three inches shorter, solidly built, and deeply freckled. He grabbed a quesadilla and said in that cockles-warming idiolect, "Come here often?" I laughed despite myself, a surprise of a laugh that was more spittle and cough than anything else. McNairy laughed too. Then he became serious and motioned to a table, far from the other new fish. I followed, naturally; he set his tray down and said, "You're the guy from the city papers, correct? Those midtown widows?" I nodded, seeing no need to correct him—the Bearnaise is technically Upper West Side—and felt, from something in his voice, mildly flattered. "And such small hands too," he said, wrapping his thumb and index finger around my diminutive right wrist. Nobody around us said a word or even acknowledged us, my first intimation of McNairy's status. He released my wrist and leaned in. "Look, I have an eyelash below my eyelid. Right here. Can you get it out?" I needn't tell you, the second my services were requested the old doorman habits returned. I nodded and grasped McNairy's head with my right hand, hooking my thumb at his eyelid, gently pushing downward. I've had superlative dexterity as long as I can remember; it even saved my life back in Trinco with the Hilton Hotels advance man. He paid me handsomely to clear the scrub before principal construction, which meant sweeping for residual LTTE land mines, which meant the softest of soft touches while crawling the expanse between the Nilaveli beachfront and Pulmoddai Road. Of course, I'm no fool, you can only perform the job for so long before you blow off hand, leg, or face. The prudent man allays his risk while still netting maximum profits. After a week of crawling I followed my employer's lead and outsourced the labor: a hundred and thirty rupees per mine. My friends were happy to earn the money, and since the work carried a whiff of masculine/humanitarian violence, their raised stature with the nursing school students made for a most appreciated bonus.

To return: McNairy's eye watered over, and if he blinked the eyelashes would become too slippery to hold—with these things you have just one real opportunity. I spotted it at once, floating in a shallow pool between reddened sclera and the thin band of tissue. The world disappeared, with a slow pinch of my left thumb and middle finger I plucked the errant lash, and before I removed my fingers I paused, McNairy's pupil was directed straight ahead, which is to say straight ahead at me; he hadn't blinked once. It's an incredible thing how one minute people are strangers and a minute later they are friends, sometimes they are still strangers even while they are friends; and with lovers it's worse, sometimes they become strangers again, though this is not necessarily unwelcome.

That's how it was with McNairy—or, rather, how it is. Our courtship was brief, an evening or two drinking toilet wine during open call; McNairy favored a bracing variety flavored with anise: "That'll put lead in your pencil. Now you just need to find someone to write to." He told me about his side business in bleaching anuses, integral to his unique position of *protected, yet apart*. I can report it was a professional and hygienic setup, employing an off-brand gel he had smuggled in and would apply with a Popsicle stick; McNairy was very upfront about the burning. Whenever I inquired about the business, he'd shake his head and reply, "I've seen things . . ."

So have we all, my brother, so have we all. At the risk of purple prose, let me say in those moments with him I felt an openness beyond geography and beyond limit.

I would not think it a breach of privacy to share one of his more endearing traits, considering the circumstances, to record here for posterity. He'd follow his orgasm with an indecorously loud remark—"A celebration!"—said more to himself than anyone else; I don't pretend to know its origins. I do know he was, and is, a true gentleman. He never asked for my version of that night at the Bearnaise, not once, and lest you think (as I thought) this some unspoken prison code, some two-way street—with McNairy I was always learning on my feet, as it were—he volunteered his own story: robbing an off-track betting spot, fatally shooting a minor. Though he spent the first nineteen years of his life in Jersey City, he rarely visited Manhattan, and McNairy thrilled to hear my stories of life on the island. I would run a hand over the musculature in his arms and legs, tell him about, say, the hundreds of immigrant workers buried in the Statue of Liberty's crown, sacrificed during its many restorations; they just fell over and died and the guys behind them took over and worked until *they* fell over and died, and on and on. The world just consumes us and the lucky ones are cornmeal for the maw of art and the maw of beauty, dying in the service of something greater than ourselves.

Which is not to say it was all wine and roses: I do not wish to give a false impression of our relationship. We argued like any other couple, about communication, about making time for each other. Plus he harbored suspicions of Betsy from the start. I'd thought it was simple jealousy; of course now I realize it was simple deductive reasoning. He'd screw up the courage after hitting the booze, saying I'd gone soft, cunt-blind. Then he would collapse onto his bed slab—he slept with the mattress folded against the wall, said he didn't like to get too comfortable—and I remember once he sighed, "Compassion, Jesus Christ, how inefficient. It's exhausting, compassion." We were strong, though, we are strong, and we would make up every time and on special occasions break out the pop rocks. McNairy, you taught me so much! With a swell of *surabondance* in my chest I dedicate my literary corpus to you.

I see my outpouring of feeling has engendered the same in many of you, judging by the upvotes in Reddit's r/mcnairyfanfic. I thank all of you for your support, your enthusiasm, and your—how to put it?—imagination. It appears as though #westbrookriot isn't trending as highly as it was this afternoon; it's to be expected, we're approaching hour five, even Bollywood films have intermissions. What else is being served at tonight's entertainment buffet? On Fox News you have "Stepdad Rescues Daughter from Teacher," "Tiger Man of Utah (VIDEO)," and "Small-Town Parade Disaster (VIDEO) (NSFW)." The cornucopia of life in these United States, it's quite beautiful. Let us never take a single moment for granted.

Though it would be opportunistic and distasteful to appropriate this riot for my own purposes, it must be said that people are dying out there and it's important to make the best of it.

Yes, that was my hand; I know WBCS camped outside of the Media Center hoping for such a moment. The glass was cool to the touch despite the humidity inside; with my arm fully outstretched I could lay my palm flat against its surface, an almost penitential gesture from which I admit deriving a foreign pleasure, a foreign and childlike pleasure. Let the high-def image of my hand be my final portrait, my synecdochic *adieu*. (The Warden had the iMacs' webcams disabled.) The same hand that pulled *The Holding Pen* out of the muse's birth canal and into the light, the same hand that slapped *The Holding Pen* to beckon its first cry and gauge its respiratory response. A cry, if I may be so bold, that will ring out for decades hence. And more immediately, my hastily scrawled "Free Mumia" sign has spread with the visibility of a thousand billboards . . . Three minutes later, we're once again atop and astride the national conversation.

Ah, yes, but for how long? Like everyone, in idle moments I've contemplated my own death, dramatized it in the cinema of my mind. As a teenager it was a melodramatic image, dying in the arms of my lover in the Galle Fort, my body riddled with bullets. At the Bearnaise I had plenty of time to envision a new scene, one with the detail and fastidiousness of one of those Brueghels at the Met: I would fall from a great height, seeing the world as the birds do, as our kind was never meant to. I wondered and do wonder if I would glean some particular insight before I hit the pavement—I always envisioned an urban setting—something approaching total clarity. Most often I crashed through the roof of an idling taxi, if only for the comic potential of the driver to perfunctorily reply, "Where to?" (You have to give people levity amidst the tragedy.) As you have likely suspected: Yes, I always chose the Bearnaise for my launching pad, as it were; that's only natural, and besides, I'm not very creative.

Those idle hours at the podium made the transition to Westbrook relatively painless. For four years I was 3 West Seventy-Second Street's consummate doorman, the custodian and sentry for a storied address built with Carnegie money in 1928, rehabbed by Halston in 1976, and managed by a Saudi-based holdings company since 2009. While its residents were almost exclusively among the most well-heeled bankers and captains of industry, the Bearnaise was not without a bit of spice in the stew, as they say. Jerzy Kosinski lived in 9F in the late 1970s, holding afternoon debates in the lobby and carrying on late-night assignations with Ms. Klatten. It's said the lobby ashtrays had to be emptied every twenty minutes.

Any old fool can be a doorman. I was the *greatest* doorman, going above and beyond to ensure total comfort for the septuagenarian and octogenarian and, in the case of Ms. Beales, nonagenarian women of the Bearnaise. Many of our residents' husbands had fulfilled their actuarial duties in predeceasing these ladies; I quite preferred the widows, truth be told.

Total comfort meant knowing where to unload the Gristedes bags in every kitchen in every apartment. Total comfort meant remembering which grandchildren Ms. Rothschild spoiled and which grandchildren to send away. (If only I'd known to block that GSSR conscript!) Total comfort meant cooing at Ms. DeWitt's purchase of a Givenchy toddler's bib, the same one she'd purchased four days previous, and would again purchase four days hence. Total comfort meant directing Ms. Hwang's visitors through the maid's door, as her site-specific Richard Serra barred entrance from the main foyer. Total comfort meant retrieving a battered old TV from the hallway closet in 303 and setting it on the upholstered Louis XIV chair so Ms. Miyake-Burns could watch *The Price Is Right* reruns and exhale lusty gutturals at Bob Barker's face—she reserved impotent moues for the contestants who overbid on common household items like combination washer-dryer units and vacuum cleaners with attachments for hard-to-reach places. Ms. Miyake-Burns once confided she had frequent nightmares about appearing on the show and overbidding on herself: she was both contestant and product, speculating wildly amid vociferous suggestions from the audience. Every weekday morning I'd return at 9:30 to hoist the TV back into the closet.

Some of the other doormen, particularly James on second shift, they avoided Ms. Miyake-Burns whenever possible. She was curt, it must be said, but I believe it was her past that put everyone on edge. She was the rare self-made widow in the Bearnaise, or anywhere really, alone at forty after an embolism blossomed in her husband's skull one day at the trading desk. My white-collar readers likely recognize the name MB Holdings; Ms. Miyake-Burns was the eponymous head of the organization, something of a pioneer for creating a futures market in liberal outrage. (Her oft-quoted line: "I give Goldman a reason to expense their *Times* subscription.") Her prescient decision to divorce it from the major exchanges meant she could incorporate 501(c)3 nonprofits, which later fueled a good chunk of activity and fees. As you can imagine, Ms. Miyake-Burns frequently nudged the Bearnaise staff for ideas, truffle hunting through the scandals of the day for the revelations with real staying power. I quite enjoyed it, though James called it financially vampiric, the obverse to that Joe Kennedy tale of exiting the market after receiving stock tips from shoeshine boys.

I remember the spring evening she returned from a Bloomberg gala, award in hand; she invited me up to watch TV with her, I thought why not, it was after eleven and the building pretty much retired by 9:00 p.m., we passed a pleasant thirty minutes or so watching Turner Classic Movies. Before she fell asleep on her settee, her slim frame weighed down by a Lanvin pendant necklace, Ms. Miyake-Burns pointed to the TV and whispered, "The actor who plays that horse is dead now."

I've read enough biographies inside to know how little interest any of this holds, I cannot fault your flagging attention. We only wish to know the story behind why a known personage is known at all, if you will, without all the preamble. Everyone comes from somewhere, which is another way of saying everyone comes from nowhere; it's just plain uninteresting, I agree. And yet, and yet: my years at the Bearnaise are as much a part of me as *The Holding Pen*, even if the latter has brought me this readership and infamy (and the former brought me nine consecutive life sentences). As much as I intend this final issue to be my apologia and *an official accounting of events, as they happened*, I must also be true to my own higher calling, and hope you'll excuse a detour into autobiography.

I remember the smells of the Bearnaise, those return first, the ladies doused in perfume to ward off the decrepitude; they really poured it on for charity galas and visits to their geriatrician, usually a Max von Sydow type with an office on Park, I'd hold open a taxi door and inhale a fog of bergamot and ambergris. The scent hung in the lobby for hours, resistant to the mini-fan we kept behind the redwood podium, it bonded to the skin under the livery, and good luck trying to lose it with exercise or after-work beers. I wonder how much the olfactory barrage contributed to my bachelorhood: it was like carrying around a rodent drowned in patchouli oil; I'm sure I triggered many a memory of incontinent grandparents for whoever was unlucky enough to stand near me. This was all well before I'd awoken my artistic temperament, mind you, which I now know is sexual catnip. As Steve Martin said, it's all about timing. I don't think it a stretch to say the contours of my life back then fit closely to that of my job: the job was everything, you see; I preferred it that way. Did I want for entertainment? From my Bearnaise post I could watch the entire world go by, and since it was Manhattan, the entire world did go by: tourists with their slow zigzags, one in four stopping to ask for directions; junior analysts walking three abreast in iceberg-blue dress shirts and tropical wool slacks, wolfing down burritos on their lunch break, with their sweaty cheeks it looked like something being birthed backwards; Hispanic construction crews debating *fútbol* and ferrying ladders and buckets, the neighborhood under constant restoration; Jamaican nannies and their charges in military-grade strollers, both of them wearing headphones; and the women, the women! It was all I could do to restrain myself from relief in the doormen's coat closet, which I only resorted to a half dozen times, or now that I think of it more a baker's dozen. Most often I'd look up and exhale through my mouth in a silent whistle; I'd look up and count the window A/C units on the Chatsworth across the street, little silver knuckles running up the stories.

I suppose what attracted me to the job is the simple truth that the liveried doorman is not an individual, and this is as it should be. It was thrilling to take a nine-hour vacation from myself to become pure function inside a well-weathered apparatus. That apparatus, thankfully, came wrapped in romantic delusion. Look to the classic American films of the 1940s and there we are: quiet, solicitous, taking Ms. Kelly's bags, Ms. Hepburn's bags. A white-gloved helping hand for the postwar magnates and their wives and children. We dialed their Dr. Feelgoods through the proletariat panic of the 1970s, their fixers in the S&L crisis of the 1980s, their Eastern Bloc party girls in the go-go 1990s.

The court-appointed psychiatrist later told me I should have been troubled by the thrill I derived from anonymity. I suppose for others it was more difficult to wear the costume of self-effacement, whereas I could remain stock-still at my perch for hours, gazing into the middle distance like a dutiful statuary. One night, after returning from a midshift tipple at O'Malley's, I swear my head detached from my body and floated around the lobby like a balloon, without agency or direction. I consulted James. He'd put in the time, surely he could relate. I don't recall his response exactly, but the gist was: Everyone thinks they're a fake. Everyone's lying constantly. No one gets caught. The lies are too complex to determine guilt, let alone any kind of reckoning. Calm down and stop worrying so damn much. James then went into a short rant about the lack of reckoning in society as a whole, epitomized by the recent drug scandals at the Scripps National Spelling Bee. I stopped listening and wondered instead how he might react if I pulled my dick out of my trousers and urinated on his shoes. I experienced many of these fugitive thoughts, more so near the end of a shift.

I see that bang-trimmed Mata Hari is taking live interviews with her dashcam, one of four talking heads on MSNBC, fielding tough questions like "How are you holding up?" Worse yet, her chyron identifies her as "Betsy Pankhurst, Author," likely the work of her opportunistic publicist and, if you'll forgive the nit-picking, only true in the technical sense. She is a destroyer, one joined on-screen by state senator Nina Vasquez, filmmaker Frank Darabont, and supermax architect Leonard Goodwin. I can see over Betsy's shoulder a bit of highway signage spinning outward, as if in orbit; she must be rounding the exit 70 off-ramp. I know it is self-defeating to check in on her, to hear her voice crack as she tells Joe Scarborough, "My partner and I believe in love, we believe in justice, and we believe in America. This catastrophe is a total rejection of those beliefs and of those who share them." I resolve to never again mention her spirit-draining obloquy. It is at best a distraction.

Despite my outsize imaginative capacity, I have no idea what Betsy will do upon her arrival.

I feel lucky to be granted the chance to "say good-bye," as it were, before the quick and violent end. Well, an end sure to be violent, less sure to be quick. Either way it's preferable to how the English satirist Jonathan Swift went out. He possessed a life-long fear of aphasia, which he paid little mind—everyone thought he'd expire a young man, slain by one of his many enemies, Swift even carried a sidearm in response to the death threats (that may have been Pope; in fact, now that I think about it, I'm sure it was Pope); wouldn't you know it, a stroke is exactly what befell the man. It would be funny in other circumstances: for the last five years of his life, Swift was bedridden and mute. To that I say, No thank you. Swift must have known the touch of history was upon him—or, rather, History—very few of us ever feel it, and those who do must profess a modest ignorance after the fact. Instead we resort to cliché: we were "in the zone" sinking that championship-winning shot or pulling that comrade from the flaming wreckage.

The touch of History is unmistakable. It starts as a cold scrotal grip, alarming and, at the same time, strangely pleasant. History cannot be confused with any other sensation, it travels up the urethra and pelvis, an armada of pinpricks, thousands of them, decidedly foreign but not unwelcome; all whispering, "You are part of something larger."

Where was I? Ah, yes, the Bearnaise. I alternated between the second and third shifts, I had no real control over my schedule due to a lack of seniority in the union coupled with the flexibility of what the IRS would call Single Income No Dependents. I'd clock out and change into civilian clothes in the discreet coat closet/storage space to the right of the entrance, its walls, I remember, lined with portraits of Bearnaise staff past and present, dot-matrix printouts of FedEx and UPS timetables, and an instructional poster on the Heimlich. Whether my shift ended at 4:00 p.m. or midnight, my custom remained the same: sidle up to O'Malley's on Sixty-Fifth, order a Lion Lager from the gruff barkeep, Mick or Brian or Buddy, I can't remember; I'd drink my beer slowly, waiting for it to warm to room temperature, as Rajit and I drank it in Trinco. On the weekends, when the house band played—a folk-inspired three-piece named Orange You Glad I Didn't Say Banana—I would forgo the bar for long walks across the island, threading the cement expanse of Lincoln Center to the Hudson, as if my ingrained compass always pointed to the nearest body of water. I would say I was alone with my thoughts, but in truth I don't believe I thought anything at all. I do remember one August night, it may have been one or two a.m., I was startled by the cracking-wood sound of a horse-drawn carriage speeding down an empty Central Park West, an outsize, ship-tossed din. I turned as a deranged horse marauded past me, the carriage rocking on its axle like a glass about to topple, and the carriage driver giving chase two blocks behind, then three. As the horse sped by at what I guessed was full gallop, I searched his expression for . . . Bridled joy? Rabies-fueled exultation? The horse was, ultimately, inscrutable. And in the face of such newfound freedom—itself a form of terror—such an expression might be deemed equine courage. Yes: I deem it.

Even now I long to escape this room and do nothing more than stroll the west lawn. I would approach the WXHY Action News team and the WBCS news team and give a reassuring pat on the back to the cameramen, a manly pat on the back with a squeeze of the shoulder that says, *We're all in this together,* and also says, *You're doing good work here,* and also says, *Wow, that camera must be heavy.* I would walk to the tree line and slow my pace, absorbing the details. I can imagine the leaves mottled by caterpillars, the darkness beyond shading to reveal a muddy glen strewn with fallen branches and ancient beer bottles. All that earth roiling underfoot! I would bend down with the ease of a potato farmer and run my hands through the dark loam, releasing fertile odors. I would nod approvingly, as if some test had been passed, as if I were on camera, as if I had any part in such a beautiful place. I would stand up, part the branches, and step inside.

It is not to be. While Diosito and his cohorts raid Taghkanic's cheese shop Mon Oncle, while the GSSR and the Appeals elevate their rival chanting—Godspeed! I wish them luck traversing the swamp of protest rhetoric—while the riot expands with inexorable progress: I will sit here and die. (Or, not *just* sit here and die. Jumping jacks keep the blood pumping.) If I may take one measure of solace, it is that my death will become an extratextual coda to Betsy's book, rendering much of its power obsolete, or at the minimum incomplete, by the major news of the day. Today. My day.

Wonders never cease: WXHY Action News is interviewing Warden Gertjens. The wily bastard got out after all. He looks freshly showered and shaved, his trademark turtleneck and clear plastic glasses conveying a mastery of the situation: he's the king of his castle. The castle may be stormed by peasants and partly afire, but it remains his castle. He's responding to field correspondent Jay Minh, something about "a national tragedy" and "the exigent demands for building stronger china shops for ever stronger bulls," plus a spurious disquisition on Westbrook's historical dedication to safety. If you'll excuse the digression, I've heard stories from the grizzled veterans contradicting the Warden's claims. There was the rash of inmate suicides in the mid-1950s, a response to the widespread use of extended solitary and abandoned only after concerns voiced by the governor's wife after her tour of the grounds. There was the rookie screw who slipped LSD into everyone's soup in 1972; the entire population lay supine for hours, unable to be roused from their trips. Or—and this is decidedly apocryphal—the whispers of decommissioned land mines buried in the weed-choked knolls to the northeast, an escape deterrent dreamed up by the late Warden Brown in the booming postwar years. This particular bugaboo persisted for decades, in the way such idiocy does, belying the institutional logic of Westbrook: How would a cash-strapped warden have ramrodded such an improvident use of funds? And given the odd spike in escapes from 1955 to 1959, wouldn't there be articles in *The Times Union* of exploding prisoners? (A search of the paper's digital archives yields only a few results, mostly about Communists on our board of directors.) Any actual land mines would have detonated hours ago with all the trampling about by the WBCS camera team, the *Fox News Live at 5* crew, the Appeals, the GSSR, the food trucks, and what appears to be the *quinceañera* of an inmate's niece or daughter. They better get their portraits in early: the forecast predicts nighttime precipitation. Even now the sky is darkening with thick scud clouds; on any other day this kind of weather would send a nerve of excitement through Westbrook. I suppose it's part of the magical thinking so common to prison life, rising baro-metric pressure sets the lifers gossiping about nor'easters off the Atlantic. Everyone daydreamed about twisters obliterating screw nests, hurricanes sweeping through with a liberating menace—hell, even the April sunshowers got us excited.

Red, blue, and yellow lights are flashing brighter through the high windows, it must be the wagon circle of ambulances and fire trucks, blinking just a hair from syncopation. A strong part of me wishes it would fall into a comfortable pattern, though, yes, I know, that would defeat its purpose, but we all know we'll be here for a while. Or at least they will. I hopped up just now to get a look at the cordon, there are indeed a half dozen fire trucks, long vehicular muscles ready for flexing. I wonder why they aren't attending to the fires in A and B Blocks. Perhaps something to do with protocol, or maybe insurance? There is a kind of beauty to idling in an emergency, a rejection of what's expected, I suppose, it's a minor rebellion I can certainly endorse and would argue is not so dissimilar to the entire feeling of youth.

I admit to mixed feelings about Warden Gertjens's survival. I know I should not wish ill on my patron and benefactor. And yet History demands blood. Shall I be the sole martyr today? Must my body be the only one laid atop the funeral pyre of postpenal literature? I suppose what bothers me most is the lack of contri-tion in Warden Gertjens's voice. If he's blind to his own role in this world-shaking moment, so be it. If he looks on the storming of the Bastille as mere property damage, so be it. *The Holding Pen* is worth a riot, worth a hundred riots. This work will outlive us all, it will outlive us all and gather momentum and be taught to schoolchildren and recited at the commencement of major sports events. Yes, certainly, it is worth my own life, on this random Tuesday, as I type with cramping fingers and a bouncing knee in the Will and Edith Rosenberg Media Center for Journalistic Excellence in the Penal Arts.

Do I exaggerate? I've studied the trends, I know the troubled passage all new art faces on its path to canonization. There's a first blush of popularity, followed by a gauntlet of criticism most often directed at the fallibility of its creator. I will fare easier than most, my sins are well documented, my incarceration is itself a rubber-stamped takedown. What can the critics say about me that isn't immediately obvious? I'm not in denial of the things I've done. When I returned to my post that night at the Bearnaise, I did so with complete sangfroid, manning my station with professionalism; I even took care to wipe the perspiration from my forehead and the back of my neck with a handkerchief spritzed with rosewater. And when Ms. Hwang's son stopped by—his office at Barclays was about twenty blocks south—I greeted him with courtesy and with the subtlest genuflection. (The picture cracked, as it were, when he returned to the lobby and burst from the elevators screaming into his phone, "You better fucking be here when I hang up and you better fucking find out what happened to my meemaw!")

The WXHY Action News interview with Warden Gertjens has cut away to footage from inside, it appears one of the Appeals' smartphones made it in after all. The picture quality is quite poor, either from backlighting or the increasing amount of smoke in the flats. And quite shaky, too, the phone is being fought over with a chorus of offscreen requests: "Lemme send my girl a dick pic first, then you can have it"; "M13, aye aye aye!"; "Jamal, Jamal, turn that shit over here, get it on me." The camera swings around to Frankie holding a bleeding white guy in a headlock, the two of them splayed out like Greco-Roman wrestlers. Frankie is beaming with hard-won pride, his sparring partner's face is pocked and bruised to the hilt, as if sculpted from masticated cherry pits. Frankie is slapping the man's forehead, repeating, "Say it. Say it and I'll let go. Say it." The camera zooms in to Frankie's face, or rather it isn't a zoom, something has sent the phone flying toward him, it hits Frankie square in the forehead, the picture goes dark. The phone must still function, however: next we hear O'Bastardface's bellowing drawl, "I didn't come here to make friends. I came here to win!" It's unclear where in Westbrook this is taking place. I spotted the blue-and-white floor stripes demarcating the inmate and screw walk lanes, so they're in the central corridors, likely between C and D Blocks and the row of solitary cells at the entrance to E Block. Close. It's no relief to hear O'Bastardface in such high spirits. This is his New Year's party: the clinking glass, collisions with strangers, old acquaintances not forgotten, a revived (and abusive) *bonhomie*. I would prefer to see anyone else break through my meager barricade. O'Bastardface has always put me at unease; McNairy once remarked, "That guy took a chain saw to his mental furniture long ago." Perhaps O'Bastardface's greatest flaw is an inability to simply rest, to *be*, something I learned during a routine keeplock a few months back—March, perhaps: a screw found a sharpened toothbrush, it was a day in the cell for everyone. The inspections ate up a.m. work detail, which begat boredom, which begat cursing out the screws because, well, everyone was bored. I decided to use the time productively and plot out feature ideas for the gaps in Volume I, Issue Ten ("Paradise"). Colleagues in the industry recognize the necessity for long lead times, which doesn't really apply to *The Holding Pen*, but I instituted them anyway to maintain a sense of professionalism with Warden Gertjens and, truth be told, a sense of professionalism with myself. The policy also gave me a handy excuse with the more aggressive pitches: Sorry, would love to do a profile on your melamine-board sculpture from the woodshop, but the issue's full.

Two hours into keeplock I heard a primitive, ominous gurgle and turned to find my morning deposit rising up to greet me. As I leapt up onto my bunk I heard cries of disgust along the galley; at least I wasn't alone in this plumbing *bête noire*, the puddle spread past my cell to meet its sibling coming out of O'Bastardface's cell, his boisterous cackle identified his own toilet as our fecal estuary: he'd flushed his bedsheet. The insults shouted his way— "Motherfucker, I'm kill you for this," "Last time I get shit on my felon flyers," "I was napping, goddammit"—only fed his laughter more. The brackish film spilled across the flats and pooled around the shallow concavity at south gate. (I learned my cell rested at the bottom of a shallow decline.) Screws bounded out of the gates, undeterred by the splashing their footfall sent upward and out. From what I could hear O'Bastardface welcomed their blows with the equanimity of a conscientious objector—he knew fighting back would result in a longer bout of solitary.

As I said, O'Bastardface is the last person I would want interrupting my final and *official accounting of events, as they happened.*

And yet I must pause for a moment to marvel at how long I've been allowed to commune with you, my friends and mass confidants. It's been roughly six hours since the beginning of the riots—if we grant riots even have a "beginning," I could argue we've "always" been rioting—and I'm feeling, knock on wood, something approaching hopeful. This could end at any moment, I know, and lest we forget the Buddha says we're all already dead, but it hasn't ended yet, and I have so much still to share with you, with the historical record, before the blunt-force trauma, before the end.

And yet this nape-hair anxiety is quite draining. I'm reminded of the evening after a second shift at the Bearnaise, it was midnight or one a.m., I was idling on the Uptown 3 platform. As the train approached, two hands grasped my shoulders from behind and pushed me forward—a white starburst filling my vision and mind—and just as quickly the hands pulled me back. I turned to see three black kids hooting and backslapping as they raced up the stairs. I laughed, too, a broken laugh like the sputter of a boat engine, drawing stares from my fellow subway riders, a broken laugh that dissolved into shaking and light pants wetting.

That was merely a second of anxious doom; this is a marathon. Exhaustion has set in. Perhaps even boredom. Okay, okay: I hear you, I hear you and I see your subtweets implying ingratitude. And though my own demise is assured, and will be understood by generations of scholars as a fitting coda to my editorial project—"He gave it his all"—my E Block neighbors would shake their heads. The arc of time does not bend toward justice. How could it? Justice is an abstraction. These carceral commons, if you'll allow a subjective bias, is an animal place, with the thinnest veneer of civilization, a semitransparent veneer through which I've spied the truth, through which—to borrow a phrase from my psychotropic-drug-addled friends in C Block—I've "seen through the bullshit." The arc of time bends toward nothing save for time itself.

Is that whistling I hear? There's a teakettle register somewhere down the hall, though it might not be human—a pinched heating duct, perhaps—and yet I shudder at the sound of an approaching malefactor. The sound is continuous, neither rising nor descending, and I wonder, perhaps foolishly, if it is an ally, or if not an ally then a nodding acquaintance, also squirreled away and riding this thing out. He wouldn't have the writing of this *official accounting of events, as they happened* to bide his time, and may be at this moment finally reduced to the self-annihilating moth light of his plaintive whistle. In which case, my heart goes out to you, my friend or rather, my acquaintance, my heart goes out to you with sympathy and empathy, for I, too, would not wholly protest the day's end, nor all that is implied by it. However, and this may carry a whiff of hypocrisy, if the whistling is coming from someone around the corner, biding his time, arms akimbo and playing what he thinks to be mind games—which, if true, I admit are more effective with each passing minute—then I do wholly protest the day's end and all that is implied by it. I am not ready, I haven't even gotten to the trial, nor the *Holding Pen* Amex card—0.5 percent of purchases donated to a legal defense fund for contributors—I am not ready at all, I need more time, and, yes, I acknowledge the sly wink from the universe: time is the one commodity I've had in abundance all these Westbrook months and years. And yet, if I were to be accorded another hour, another twenty minutes, such time would be invaluable for future scholars of postpenal lit. Not to mention present ratings for the local news.

I am not above requesting a distraction from my brothers-in-arms. The Appeals have shown blush-inducing solidarity; now is the time to, as they say, "kick things up a notch." My brothers might engineer some kind of chaos near A Block and drive the crowds east and away from the Media Center . . . ?

The whistling's subsided; it drew down steady and measured, perhaps a mechanical softening or a practiced human one. Either way: downright chilling.

As I said, I am not ready. With the end in sight *The Holding Pen* may not have its own end, which is to say by the very circumstance of its creation this final Editor's Letter will be interrupted, not finished. As everyone knows, that which is unfinished is also without end, and that which is without end cannot be a work of literature. I now realize, with distress and a new valence of panic, this confession may very well upend my literary corpus, may upend it and destroy it, like a hiccup-filled eulogy. Was it better to depart in silence, to never have even started this *official accounting of events, as they happened*? I'm sweating from the distress and the panic, which have redoubled, and not from the broken A/C or the low-lying fear of death; it is the sweat of destiny, or a destiny thwarted, a stumble across the proverbial finish line and an end in personal and public ignominy. How did I not think of this before? I curse sophomore Alexis Somers and the auto-publish feature, all these words I cannot recall from the digital ether.

And yet: I continue. I seem to always do this—that is, to start something without a sense of the ending, a sense of where it will take me, if I may disassociate for a moment. Some people, as Mc-Nairy would say, are just poor planners.

Perhaps it is not so dire, now that I think on it. The inevitable blunt caesura of this final Editor's Letter will perfectly mirror my own blunt end, a rather unique and unrepeatable rhetorical flourish—take that, Fritz!—not dissimilar from the hostage diary or the suicide note. I welcome the extreme pathos.

Ah, I see #rememberthepen is trending. It fills my heart to bursting to see your links to treasured stories and poems and topical cartoons. To be honest—to continue my honesty streak—I had forgotten about some of the earlier pieces. There's fan favorite "Yr People" from Volume I, Issue Three ("Badlands"), which began Lewis Atwell's stellar run from *The Holding Pen* to *Harper's* to *Kinfolk*. One of our few science-fiction pieces—considered "light SF" by adherents and not "light sci-fi," never anything "sci-fi," it's like saying "San Fran" to Haight-Ashbury habitués—Atwell's story posits a post-diluvian Manhattan and a new southern border of 125th Street. A city councilwoman and proud Harlemite confers with the old heads about an immigration policy to contend with the Upper East Side crowds knocking at their door, proffering Birkin bags in exchange for potable water. Did I tear up at Anita's extended dream sequence, where her nostalgia for our present commingles with lyrics from Bobby Womack's immortal "Across 110th Street"? I may have, I may have.

Naturally the millennial set is rallying behind Jin-ho Yoo's story "AAAAAH OH," which many discovered through the *Best American Nonrequired Reading* anthology, guest edited by Kristen Wiig (thanks Kristen!). At the risk of offending our young readers I confess I did not initially understand the story. I consulted with Warden Gertjens, who thought the many references to Urban Outfitters might flatter the company into carrying *The Holding Pen*—this was perhaps three issues before they picked us up—and when I expressed my doubts he pulled rank and demanded its publication. Well, I'm not too proud to admit when I'm wrong, and Warden Gertjens's insight brought us a vital, underrepresented voice. Hundreds wrote to say they identified with the story's disaffected young protagonist: they, too, have pawned their roommates' jewelry for ketamine; they, too, have wandered the NYU campus for whole days; they, too, have seen the faux-vintage T-shirt in UO with the phrase "Funk Seoul Brother" and realized they never replied to their mother's voice mails about their recently departed father. They, too, have then taken more ketamine and posted ten-thousand-word L=A=N=G=U=A=G=E poetry on Facebook.

Were I to pick a favorite, an essentially impossible task, the first that comes to mind would be "The Poet" by Cesar Rojas, a middleman among the Latin Kings, an absolute prizefighter among prose stylists. Who could forget his rhetorical riddles and evasions? A poet in Cartagena is to give a reading at the local university, he decides to recite his friend's verses instead, perhaps as a joke, perhaps as a test of the critics; his friend even attends the reading and never realizes the theft, as it were, even compliments him afterward over steak and red wine. The poet goes farther, he sleeps with his friend's wife, does so in such a bald-faced manner, nobody is surprised when they are caught *in flagrante delicto*—except, presumably, the friend's wife—and most remarkably the friend does nothing, he does nothing and says nothing. This enrages the poet, who follows him and yells, "Why aren't you upset? Do something!" The friend just smiles. Meanwhile, the critics are saying the poet has turned a corner, entered a new frontier in Colombian letters. The poet is at the height of his career and in the nadir of his life, he develops insomnia and high blood pressure, his friend's maddening equipoise is killing him, and while complaining to his nephew the two hatch a plan to mug his friend, to catch him unawares and savor the look of fear on his face. Naturally they're both arrested midrobbery, the poet ends up in jail, and his friend visits him every week.

I see the upper window in the Media Center is stippled with rain, and visibility has dropped to a hundred feet or so. On the southern lawn news crews have brought out their mobile klieg lights, forming a high corona of pale white above the dots of yellow from the Appeals' flashlights and the GSSR's battery-powered fluorescents—or perhaps it is the Appeals' battery-powered fluorescents and the GSSR's flashlights: my view is streaked by the rain and an uptick in activity. Instagram shows a few portraits in close detail: Bronwen Taylor and the Cornell PhD candidate in matching bandanas, facing the camera with tongues out and left hands curled in the universal "Hang loose" sign; a kimchi taco from one of the food trucks, tagged #bestever and #foodporn; the smoke rising from B Block, reflected upside-down inside a large puddle; a bikini-clad woman on a beach exhorting the viewer to trade likes for followers. There's a whiff of petrichor in the air near the window, a welcome change from the sulfurous and dried-urine scent I've grown accustomed to; I would not have guessed until this very moment how much I valued and do value last smells. The necrotic perfume of the riot has been filling the hall, I can almost see it, though that may be fatigue setting in; still, you encounter all sorts of new odors inside, I remember Cornrow from D Block, a quiet old-timer and hall-of-fame molester, he would shuffle the flats with an old cigar box clutched to his chest at all times. I saw him bite White Gerry's pinky finger clean off during a jovial attempt to pry it away; nobody bothered Cornrow after that. When he finally gave up the ghost, Dr. Edwards discovered the cigar box contained tightly rolled Ziploc bags of feces. Presumably Cornrow's, though really who knows.

I realize with surprise and a bit of shame that in the past six hours I have yet to get into the meat of my confession and *official accounting of events, as they happened.* The *tête-à-têtes* with Warden Gertjens over paper stocks. The lost "Portfolio" issue of prisoners' drawings and sketches. Hell, my first week in New York City, freshly bribed visa in hand—courtesy of the Hilton Hotels advance man, true to his word—marveling at all the people, all the faces, all the loneliness.

Betsy's now on *Anderson Cooper 360°*, the low resolution of her dashcam doing nothing to obscure her beauty, even now I must remark, despite my warring feelings about her traitorous past and traitorous present; I would not be surprised if she had stopped for a blowout before taking to the airwaves—though, if I am charitable, she has always had what women refer to as "great hair."

She is telling Anderson, "Anderson, the story today is not about

the security of our prisons, it's about the security of our borders."
That old sawhorse. Now she's courting the conservatives—they
buy more books—and Anderson is wearing his usual stone face,
always a pro, but he's giving her extra time, this one's a livewire
and he knows it (such a pro), he's forming a response when her
feed cuts out. Now, the cell service up here is quite spotty, the
screws carp about it constantly, it's one of their top three complaints after the low pay and the postseason performance of the
Buffalo Bills.

I'm not one for deathbed conversions, if I'm honest with myself I'm not one for much of anything; still, there is a frisson of
karma, especially as it's followed by a piercing exclamation from
the south lawn, a guttural exhalation into a megaphone like a
downshifting semi or a punk band's blown-out amp. When I
hopped up to the outside window to investigate the source, I
could just make out a fistfight between the Appeals and the GSSR,
a real bench-clearing brawl; the news crews loosened the grips on
their tripods to swing their cameras around, one cameraman ran
straight into the fracas with the self-sacrificing determination of a
Navy SEAL. Kudos to WXHY, they alone intuited a medium shot
was best—not too sensational, not too self-consciously framed.
The rain doesn't show up on air, but it's really coming down,
everybody's doffing makeshift ponchos save for Bronwen Taylor,
his white button-down stuck to his lean frame, the hem flapping
around with the motion of his karate moves; I can't determine the
school or tradition. I would have thought the Cornell PhD student would be fighting back-to-back with Taylor, trading quips
along the lines of "Looks like shit just got real," but no, he leapt
into the WXHY Action News Van, and—ah, I see, he's crazed

with revenge, some things you can tell by body language alone, even through the rain, even at a hundred yards. The Cornell PhD student careened through the Appeals' base camp, doing very little to be what Ms. Hwang would call a considerate driver, I counted two bystanders and one craft-services table waylaid by his recklessness, his recklessness and speed—that Action News Van sure has some pep. Naturally he made a beeline for the Media Center; naturally the tower screws quickly shot out his tires. The van slowed to a crawl just outside the inner fence line, a most unenviable position; he opened the door, the screws volleyed a few lighthearted rounds at the mud, he closed the door. Then he pulled out his phone, he read something . . . and slumped down in resignation.

He never really had a chance, he must have known as we all must know, as old Lopez said that day in the yard. I don't admit to feeling sympathy for the Cornell PhD student, perhaps just empathy—a big step forward for me, as Dr. Edwards would attest. The Cornell PhD student is boxed in, though perhaps not for long. His vehicular outburst broke the collective fever, and the two dozen state police are finally beginning their advance, with, I'm proud to say, a few of the Appeals in their wake. Everyone's streaming into Times Square, it's all riot shields, fog, and rainfall, maybe a few souvenirs for the fans.

Dear reader, I fear your digital entreaties ("Turn left! Turn left!") will fall on deaf ears. The state police are in the middle of the scrum, in the middle and very outnumbered, I mustn't entertain thoughts of rescue. No, it looks as though they've merely expedited my demise, the noise in the hallway's picking up, including the return of that damn whistling. Looking past the computer monitor I can just make out the first wisps of black smoke.

That can't be a good sign. And yet, with this confirmation, the transition of theory into practice, one might say, outside of the Will and Edith Rosenberg Media Center for Journalistic Excellence in the Penal Arts, I find an unexpected calm about my present situation. Because me? I'm an optimist.

ACKNOWLEDGMENTS

My deep gratitude to Ira Silverberg and Marya Spence, for the rocket fuel; Justin Taylor, Scott Cheshire, and Will Chancellor, for the flashlight; Lashanda Anakwah and Clare Mao, for the assist; the Vermont Studio Center and the Millay Colony for the Arts, for the space; Paul S. Loeb, J. David Macey, Ann Putnam, and Steve Cwodzinski, for the wattage; and Summer Smith, for everything.